DAMAGED HEARTS

BOOK FOUR IN THE SAVAGE HEARTS SERIES

MARY E. TWOMEY

MARY E. TWOMEY, LLC

Copyright © 2020 Mary E. Twomey
Cover Art by Emcat Designs

All rights reserved.
First Edition: November 2020

For information:
http://www.maryetwomey.com

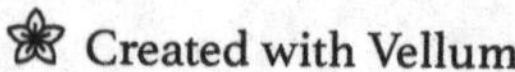 Created with Vellum

DEDICATION

To new beginnings,
And endings we put off for far too long.

DAMAGED HEARTS

Ruling with an iron fist seemed like the way to go, but when Adelita goes missing, Cruz begins to see the holes in his uncle's plans. Without stopping to check if this is a journey he's well enough to take, Cruz forsakes everything he knows to go off with Santos and Rafael in search of their missing heart.

Caring becomes contagious when Tio Bruno involves himself, giving up far too much to protect Tavita, even though there's no guarantee she's not behind Adelita's abduction.

Even though death is certain, when the warriors leave the safety of the village, they know there's no turning back.

1

NO PROTECTION
CRUZ

All my favorite things start out as bad ideas.

It was a poor choice to sleep next to Adelita, but I did it anyway. Granted, the first time, I wasn't aware she was so near, but I've invited her into my bed many nights since then, even though I knew it was dangerous.

My mother drove a stake through her own temple to escape the mental torture of La Sayona. The witch who haunted my grandfather also tormented my dad. When I came of age, La Sayona left him and seeped into me. Every night, she chases me, captures me and takes a sickle to my flesh. It's terrifying, so much that I refuse to sleep beside a woman. La Sayona is a jealous witch, zealous in her torment of our bloodline. If she senses I might be near a woman, she will drive my partner to madness.

It's why I never should have let Adelita sleep beside me.

Yet now it's my favorite thing.

Addy's soft skin brushes my face while I sleep, her midnight-colored hair tickling me when she shifts under the covers. She makes precious cooing sounds in her sleep. I know they're precious because I never use that word other than to describe her little sleep sounds.

It's an odd dichotomy of sensations that hit me when I sleep with Addy. Her curvy body looks so trusting in slumber. It makes my chest swell with all the best parts of masculine energy. I want to protect her, to buy her things, to make her smile, to hold her as if she's fragile.

Of course, she's nothing like breakable.

The other feeling I cannot deny is the overwhelming landslide of safety that engulfs me whenever I sleep by her side. I don't know what it is about her that protects me, but that's exactly what she does. La Sayona leaves me if Adelita is by my side.

My Adelita is the strongest person I've ever come across. She can tear the door off a car like it's made of tinfoil.

La Sayona should be scared.

Except tonight, she's not.

I've grown soft, too off my guard. I didn't expect La Sayona to attack tonight, but she's driven stakes into my hands, nailing me to the ground of my psyche so she can peel the skin off my back. I tell myself it's a night terror. I tell myself I'm safe, but the pain is real. Real and inescapable.

It takes a lot to wake me when La Sayona has her hold on my mind, so when water fills my nose and makes me feel like I'm drowning, I am grateful for the relief.

Santos. Santos is here. Santos is waterboarding me, because that's what he does when I can't wake up.

La Sayona screams that her pig is being taken away from her. The witch never tires of punishing the men in my family for the sins of the past.

I cough, choke and splutter as rough hands tip me onto my side. Santos is the nicest guy on the planet, but raised by sadists, so waterboarding me makes logical sense to him.

My entire nasal passage burns, but as my eyes blink the room into focus, the discomfort is the least of my problems. "What... Huh?" Why Tio Bruno is in my bedroom with Rafi and my father, while Adelita is gone is beyond me.

Santos sits back in the bed, because of course the woman of every man's dream comes with a boyfriend, who just so happens to be my adoptive brother. Santos holds his head in his hands, and when I sit up, I can see why. If his headache is anything like mine, I pity him.

The room spins while I grip the headboard. "Why are you all in my bedroom?" Then, before I can stop myself, I blurt out, "Where's Adelita?"

I'm not supposed to be this attached to her. I've tried to play it off like it was a convenience thing. She chases away La Sayona, so we sleep beside each other. No big deal. Nothing more than a friend helping out a friend.

Except I don't think friends watch each other sleep.

And I really don't think a friend notices when his buddy's nipples are taut and erect.

Shit.

"On your feet!" Tio Bruno's voice comes out like a foghorn. It's like he thinks he's still in the barracks, commanding troops and giving orders laced with unending disappointment.

If I ever found a single thing that might impress my uncle, I would do that thing every day. But as I've actually tried everything in my arsenal and he still looks at me with veiled displeasure, as he's doing right now, I'm not sure he's capable of being pleased.

My dad's cadence tempers the harsh command. "Easy, Bruno. It's clear something happened to them.

Quick, Aarón, fetch them some water. The healer's on the way. Are you hurt, boys?"

My closed eyes help me focus, but the second my lids open, the room spins again. "Ugh. Did we go drinking last night?"

Tio Bruno moves to the nightstand and sniffs our cups. "Milk. What happened? Do you know where they took her?"

"Who?"

Tio Bruno narrows his eyes at me as if he thinks I'm trying to be funny. "Adelita. Did you see who took her?" I look much like him—same shape to my mouth, same hard cut to our jawlines, same broad shoulders, thick chests and towering forms.

Only nothing about me feels towering or strong this morning. My head aches, which, after being tortured all night with a sickle, is just the icing on the cake.

I pinch the bridge of my nose, trying to force Tio Bruno's words to make sense.

Santos tilts his head up at my uncle, and then makes to stand. One step out of the bed, and his legs go out from under him. "Oh!"

Dad dashes to Santos, helping him back into the bed. "Easy, Son." He feels Santos' forehead and frowns. "He's fainted."

I gape at Santos.

Well, I'll be. He did faint.

Rafi rushes to Santos, slapping his cheeks to no avail. "Wake up! Santos, stop this! What happened?"

"Adelita? Where is she?" My mouth is so dry.

Did Adelita get up in the night and get lost on the way back to the bedroom? Is that why La Sayona was able to get to me?

Tio Bruno gets in my face and shouts, "Where is she? Who took her? Focus, Cruz!"

He's wrong. No one could possibly take Adelita. She's strong. She's...

"Cruz!" Tio Bruno barks, shaking my shoulders.

His volume combines with whatever is in my system that's making things blurry. I open my mouth to respond, but the room tilts. Before I know it, my head hits the pillow, and the room goes dark.

TWO ADELITAS
CRUZ

I'm going to be sick again. I've lost count of how often I have thrown up. I cannot imagine much more is left in me, yet every few minutes, my abdomen contracts so violently, I am certain I'll never be able to stand.

Where is she? They're not telling us anything. From the moment we woke up for the second time today, Santos and I have been vomiting worse than anything I've ever experienced.

Eva keeps knocking on the door to ask if I need water.

"Go away!" I manage, though why I'm being a jerk to her, I couldn't say. It's me I'm mad at. I had the perfect woman in my arms—in my bed, no less—and she's been snatched away from me.

At least, that's what I have been told from Tio Bruno through the door. He is angry with me because I let a daughter of Máximo go missing. But there's no way he could possibly hate me more than I loathe myself. Adelita is missing, and I can't even stand long enough to be helpful.

Eva's knock on the door is far more polite than Tio Bruno's bang, but it still irritates me. I spit into the toilet. "What?"

My sister is no shrinking violet, but I can hear her attempt to be gentle. "Santos passed out again. I just need to know you're still conscious. The healer is testing your mugs now. Aarón swears he only brought you warm milk with vanilla beans last night, but you both slept in until ten, and then passed out this morning. Now you're both barfing enough for several people. Cruz, did you two eat anything weird?"

"I had the same thing you all did at dinner, and the same thing Addy and Santos had before bed." I groan. "I don't want to talk about food."

A fresh wave hits me, and I bend over the toilet again, spewing out bile, since there is nothing left in my stomach.

Tio Bruno takes over. "Adelita, Cruz. Did you notice anyone following her?"

When the wave recedes, I gasp, clutching the seat.

"Other than the Kalku, who've been on us ever since she escaped them the first time?"

"Other than them."

I shake my head, but no one can see me. "How do you know she was taken? Maybe she ran out on me again."

I cringe at the telling language. I need to be more careful about that. She didn't run out on me. She ran out on Santos before, because she was scared the Kalku would be a danger to us.

But we brought her back home, and after we smoothed things over, she seemed happy to be with us. Granted, meeting her half-sister for the first time had been a shock, but if anything, I would guess that would make her want to stay in the village that much more.

Tio Bruno's voice lowers. "There are signs of a struggle. Blood. The front door is broken off its hinges. You were drugged, Cruz. It's the only way to explain both you and Santos sleeping through a woman being snatched right out of your bed."

Sickness weights my body, though it's not from the drug or whatever. My insides are hollow because I cannot fathom how off my guard I was to not wake up when Adelita was taken from my arms.

"The steamed milk," I guess. "The three of us had steamed milk before bed. None of you all had that."

A foggy image surfaces in my mind's eye from my dream, nagging at me to put shape to the blurs. Eva and Tio Bruno are talking to me through the door, but my aching gut tells me this picture is more important. I grab hold of it as best I can before it floats out of my reach.

"Two Adelitas," I croak, interrupting whatever instructions they are trying to give me.

"Come again?" Eva asks.

"Before La Sayona came into my mind, there were two Adelitas with me in my dream."

Eva gags. "Gross. Could you be any more of a perv? I don't want to hear about my brother's sex fantasies."

"No. One Adelita took the other away."

But Tio Bruno gets there before either of us. He swears and bangs a fist on the door to punctuate his frustration. "It's the other daughter of Máximo! I locked Tavita in the cell myself! She can't have gotten out. I'm going to check right now. Stay put. Eva, guard the door."

Tio Bruno starts shouting commands through the house, which tells me a few soldiers are milling about and springing into action. One is posted by me and Eva. One with Dad and Consuela. One with Santos and Rafi. One is sent to the sitter's house to watch my little half-siblings.

Tio Bruno's voice booms through the hallways. "Do not leave any member of the royal family unattended! If the captive daughter of Máximo is missing, then we can bet she's the one who poisoned Cruz and Santos, and abducted Adelita. No one comes in or out of this house without my say-so."

Then his boots thud toward the back door in a rush, leaving me with more questions than answers.

How could Adelita have been overpowered?

Duh, she was drugged, dummy.

Why would Tavita, Adelita's half-sister, want to abduct Adelita? When we met her last night, she didn't seem to have anything nefarious up her sleeve.

Where would she take Addy?

Realization hits me as another bout of vomit slithers up my throat.

Maybe Tavita didn't want to be rescued from the island where Máximo resides. He is her father, after all. How else would the soldiers from the Mendez tribe have made it over to the island and back, when no one else has ever managed the feat? Máximo practically giftwrapped her for them.

Tavita poisoned us so she could take our girl to the home Addy never agreed to visit.

If I had to put money on it, that she-snake is taking Adelita straight to Máximo.

Fates help us.

3

WEAK KNEES
BRUNO

I messed up. I can't even count how many ways I've miscalculated this whole thing. I shouldn't have believed that the daughter of Máximo could be trusted to stay in her cell. Who knows what kinds of tricks and weapons her wicked father showed her? She was biding her time, waiting until we brought her half-sister right to her. Not one day after Tavita met Adelita does Adelita go missing, and Tavita vanishes without a trace. The signs of struggle near the front of the house tells me Adelita fought to free herself—valiantly, in fact—but Tavita overpowered her.

I race toward the barracks, ignoring the salutes and bows that find me along the way. The people respect my authority, that's for certain, but I'm no doubt compromising that by running through the village as if I have no control over my people.

Yes, José is the chief, but this is my domain. He garners the love of the people, and I take their grave respect.

It works well for us.

I rush past the clusters of homes, the thick knots of trees, hoping I'm wrong. Maybe I'll get to the barracks and find Tavita sitting there in all of her sweetness, welcoming me to sit beside her on the cot.

Tavita. Why she wouldn't tell me her name, I'll never know. I can't shake the rose-hued image of Tavita sitting in her cell, calm and quiet, looking up at me with those damned emotional blue eyes.

I fell for her. Like a schoolboy with a crush.

Talk about a late bloomer.

But deep in my gut, I know she's gone. Cruz's hazy dream confirms what I am certain of: I underestimated the enemy. I saw the blue-eyed, silky-haired beauty and assumed she was an innocent victim.

To be fair, the soldiers from Mendez who rescued her told me that's exactly what she was. Her demeanor certainly reflected that picture. Tavita's silence was most unsettling.

She didn't fight me on being locked in her cell. On

the contrary, the locks seemed to calm her, to assure her that she was safe.

I secured her in one of the more humane cells that even had a working toilet.

How did she get out?

When my boots hit the concrete of the barracks, I slow so my knees can handle the slight downward slope. One day, I'm going to break down and admit to the healer that my joints ache, and I need something for the pain.

Not today. If I'm being honest, that's probably never going to happen. If the healers knew I had a weakness, that might spread through the village, and there goes the respect I've worked for my whole life.

I trot through the winding concrete halls, collecting the salutes of the soldiers who have no idea something is amiss.

Maybe Tavita didn't break out after all.

But as I near her cell, I know any hope that she might still be inside is foolish. Even though the door is shut, I can feel the absence of her presence. I'm loathe to admit, even to myself, that I sometimes strolled down this hallway simply because her presence calmed me. I even took to sitting in her cell in the chair at the end of long days, thinking things over and untangling my mind. She would say nothing, but just being near her helped quiet the angst everyone assumes I don't experience.

I told myself I visited her so often because a prisoner driven insane by solitude is more work in the end. But if I am being honest, I did it for myself. For that quiet calm that blanketed my anxiety.

I was weak-kneed for her, letting my insides lift the moment I walked into her cell.

Like an idiot.

It's how I know she's not inside, even as I unlock the door and tear it open. There's no sense of peace coming for me. When my eyes confirm as much, my heart sinks.

Anger rushes through my veins, as it always does when my authority is skirted. This woman escaped my cell, and it looks like she didn't use force or break through the lock. She must've stolen a key.

Like a fool, I check my belt, confirming that I am not the weak link in all of this. Relief floods me, because now I can throw my fury at someone else—whoever didn't have a hold of his keys.

I shake my head. That's neither here nor there. I've got two daughters of Máximo who have gone missing.

I make my way to my quarters and shove traveling supplies into my pack. I haven't had to go on the road in a long time, thanks to Cruz handling things outside the village. But this woman broke out of my cell and stole someone out of my brother's house. Stole Santos' girl-friend straight from his arms.

I don't care if I have to take down Máximo himself; I will not let my authority weaken because of a breach like this.

When I emerge, I go to my number two. One day, that will be Cruz, but Javier is older and a far better communicator to the soldiers. Cruz will learn, and then I can hand the army over to him. Until then, Javier is sufficient to look after things in my absence.

Javier salutes when I approach. "Morning, Commander."

I nod to acknowledge his greeting. "I have urgent business to see to. The daughter of Máximo we've had in our cell escaped in the night and abducted Adelita from Don José's home." I barely wait for the information to register with him before I push on. "I'm going to track them down and bring them back."

"Very good, Commander. How many soldiers do you need?"

Probably the whole army won't be enough to get through Máximo's wards on his island, if that's where this chase leads me. "None," I rule, which I know is fool-ish. "I'll go by myself. I might take Rafi, but I need to move quick and stay under the radar. I'm banking on the element of surprise."

It's clear by Javier's raised brows and pursed lips that he wants to argue my logic, but like a good number two, he simply nods. "If you're certain that's best."

Darn him for knowing how to talk me out of a bad idea without triggering my ego. He's one of the few who knows how to talk to me in a way to get me to listen. "You're right. Gather up a dozen soldiers. Not Cruz and the boys. They're not on their feet yet. Tavita was wearing a tracker on her ankle, so if we're quick, we can find her."

Unless she took it off.

"Very good, Commander. I'll sync her tether to your phone. And I'll look after things here while you're away."

He's fifteen years older than me, but never crosses the line by assuming he knows more than I do about how to run the army and keep the village safe. He's helpful without being overly assertive. I like Javier.

"See that you question Chef Aarón. Cruz, Santos and Adelita were poisoned with something that knocked them out, which made Adelita easier to steal in the night. I know Chef Aarón didn't do it, but see if he noticed anything off in his kitchen. If you learn anything of interest, report it to Cruz."

"Yes, Commander."

I turn on my heel and walk up the incline toward the

sunlight. Many days, I stay in the barracks because the slanted walk out is killer on my knees. I'm glad I've never admitted that to anybody.

A quick stop at the house tells me Cruz and Santos are still dealing with the poison, though at least now with the help of healers. I tell my brother I'll be gone for a few days tracking the girls, though really, it could be much longer than that.

José grips my forearm. "Bring Adelita back, Bruno. Cruz wants to marry her. She can secure our bloodline. She must be rescued. Do all you can."

My brows shoot up into my hairline. Cruz wants to marry her? Huh. He's got his work cut out for him, being that Santos dotes on her like she's an infant.

I debate snatching Rafi to go with me, but when he emerges from the bathroom Santos is in, I can see he's got sick splattered across his torso.

He's got his hands full.

I need to move now.

I leave the house to its chaos and slip out into the midmorning sun, knowing that with every minute that passes, the odds of me finding Adelita alive grow slim.

4

RACING AND RALPHING
CRUZ

Eva and Consuela help me into the car, even while they admonish me for leaving. "You're not even upright yet!" my stepmother frets, dabbing at my face with a cool washcloth.

"I don't need to be upright. Rafi's driving." Even though I have double vision from dehydration, it still smarts that I have to relinquish my hold on the driver's seat.

Eva holds onto my clammy hand, her eyes burning with unvoiced worry. She likes Adelita. She's always wanted a girlfriend her age who didn't glom onto her for her status, or talk down to her because of her frivolous fashion addiction. Addy is a good fit for her.

And now she's gone.

Aarón helped Dad pack our bags. Poor guy's been

doing everything he can to make up for the fact that someone used his drinks to poison us. It's not his fault. It's...

I still can't bring myself to say it aloud. It can't be Tavita. I looked into her eyes. I would have seen duplicity if it was in there. She was secretive, sure, but she wasn't trying to trick us. If anything, she admitted probably more than she wanted to. She gave us her name, even, and told us about Santiago.

Santos is still reeling from that. This is why we need Addy here. She'll ask the hard questions. She knows how to get people talking, even with a small tilt of her head.

"Bring my sister home," Eva says with a serious threat in her tone. Then she moves toward the driver's door, fixing Rafi with a look I cannot decipher. Eva hugs Rafi tight. "Be careful," she whispers, and I can tell she's getting choked up.

"Never," Rafi promises, like the brat he is.

She scowls, but Rafi's already rolling up his window, chuckling, though I cannot imagine what's so funny. Addy is missing. Nothing will be funny again until she's home.

I want us to get going as soon as possible, so I have to bite back a plea for Rafi to slow down when he peels out of the driveway fast enough to turn my already sensitive stomach.

Rafi blasts the music just to be a jerk. But the agony in my head doesn't last more than a few seconds before he cuts the radio to stave off Santos' groans.

As soon as I right myself, pressing my temple to the cool glass of the window, my words find me. "You're a dead man."

Rafi's laugh has a note of exhilaration to it. "I could knock you over with one hand. Save your anger for someone who's scared of you."

Santos snarls at the both of us. Though his skin is sallow and his eyes lidded, his command rings firmly through the car. "Focus, the both of you. Adelita is missing. Tavita took her, I'm guessing to bring her to Máximo. Cruz, get on your phone and call the Mendez soldiers who rescued Tavita from the island. Get as much information as you can on how they got over there. That's where we're going."

Rafi gapes at Santos. "We can't go to Máximo's island, Santos. Our best bet is to try and get to her before she crosses over there."

Santos rolls down his window to let in some fresh air. "Tavita's got half a night of a head start. Plus, she knows where she's going. We head to the island." He speaks with such certainty that neither of us argue further.

I pull out my phone, wishing there was a better plan than bold suicide. "We're not going to make it off the island if Máximo learns we've set foot on his land."

Though my words carry big implications, neither of the guys says anything to the contrary. They also don't beg off, or ask me to call for backup.

We know what we're getting into, going down this path, and we're not turning back. We'll either bring Adelita home, or we'll die trying.

I talk briefly to the me-equivalent of the Mendez tribe, listening to his short answers after he learns that we lost Tavita.

"You realize we buried two soldiers liberating her. You truly lost her?"

I bristle at his insinuation. "Thanks for your help." I end the call quickly so I don't unleash on him. "Head west, Rafi. All the way to the coast. Aim for the harbor in Chavez Park. That's where they launched out from when they went after her. We need to charter a boat at nightfall. But they said the Kalku regularly patrol the area, so when we get close, keep an eye out."

"On it."

I need to barf again, but there's no use stopping. I

roll down the window and heave over the side of the car, shaking as sweat chills on my neck and forehead.

Santos isn't far behind, his head swinging out of his window in the passenger's seat. His noises of distress tug at my heart. I'm supposed to take care of Santos. He's my responsibility. My chest aches worse than my stomach whenever he's in distress, which is saying something.

Rafi tosses a bottle of water into the backseat once I sit down. When my window rolls up, he hands me a few takeout napkins from the glove box for me to wipe off my mouth. "Maybe we should turn around," Rafi suggests.

Everything in me (which isn't much, granted) rallies at the notion that I'm not fit for a search and rescue mission. "Don't even think about it."

"Don't think about it? That's really where you're at? There are about a hundred other soldiers who are better suited for a fight than you two. Think about what's best for Adelita, not your pride."

Yet, despite his lecture, Rafi keeps driving.

Santos rolls up his window, a pathetic whine surfacing.

I double down. "By the time we get to the harbor, I'm sure the sickness will have passed."

"Or it won't, and I'll have to leave the two of you behind and cross the water by myself. You realize those are our only options, right? We don't even know what kind of poison you were given. You could be seriously in danger. Do you understand that?"

It's then that I realize Rafi isn't being belligerent. He's genuinely scared for us.

I sit up as straight as my waning energy will allow and try to convince him with my appearance that everything will be okay. Though, of course, I have no idea if that's even remotely true. Santos and I very well could be dying.

I can't think about that now. I can't be dying. Santos is a healer. He would know. He would have said something if we were.

Or he'd be an idiot, like me, and do all he could to get to Addy before our last breath.

I need to lie down. Though my body is too big for such things, I curl up on the backseat, cuddling my torso and hoping this doesn't all end in our deaths.

5

THE TRUTH ABOUT TAVITA
ADELITA

I might never be able to eat again. I cannot remember ever throwing up this much, even when I got food poisoning from some questionable goat tacos when I was a teenager. Yet no matter how much I vomit, more still comes.

"Eat another bite," Tavita urges.

"I can't!" Even crying hurts, though I can't seem to stop. "Don't make me eat!"

My sister is not aggressive, but there's no questioning I will do as she says. She's got a calm certainty to her tone that I'm guessing she gained from years of being a physical therapist, coaxing people to push themselves beyond what their bodies are comfortable doing.

Tavita's hand on my back settles my instinct to run. Not that I could stand if I tried. "The more you eat, the more you'll throw up. The poison latches onto food. The only way to get it out of your system is to give you more food and have you throw it up. It sounds weird, but that's how Father designed it."

A frustrated scream rips out of me. "Máximo is not my father! No parent of mine would ever invent something so terrible."

Tavita doesn't miss a beat. "Shh. I know." She pinches my cheeks together so my mouth pops open. Then she pushes the burrito between my teeth. When I bite down, she cups her hand over my lips so the food stays inside. "That's good. One bite at a time, we'll get this poison out of you. Have I mentioned that I'm sorry I poisoned you?"

A tear splashes into the toilet I'm kneeling before. I cannot posit a guess as to the last month that the gas station attendant cleaned the bathroom. "Why are you doing this? I still don't understand."

To her credit, she doesn't give an exasperated sigh, even though she's explained her actions at least five times on our trek.

"I didn't mean to. Please believe me. Máximo is our father, Adelita. He's as wicked as they come. When I was abducted by him, he implanted a device behind my ear. What I hear, he hears. But it only works during the day. When the moon comes out, my words are mine. That's why I didn't answer you on the drive. It's why I only wrote things down for you to read. I don't want him to hear us." She sniffles as she knots my hair in her fist. "When he sacrifices someone, he can control my actions. That's no doubt what he did last night. I saw myself sneaking into the kitchen after I heard a woman say she was going to have someone make you warm milk. I dripped the poison into the jug of milk because that's what Father made me do. I couldn't stop myself!"

Tavita waits for me to swallow and then feeds me another bite. This time, I chew on my own without needing her to coax me along.

"I can't turn around and take you back, either. If Father doesn't see you soon, he'll sacrifice someone else to control me. Our best bet is to move in the direction of the harbor, and hope Bruno finds us in time."

If it's a lie, it's the worst one I've ever heard. I know deep down that Tavita is too scared to not be telling the truth. She's been driving below the speed limit the entire way, stopping often, which doesn't fit in with an abduction.

She's stalling for time, truly hoping Tio Bruno finds us before she has to turn us over to Máximo.

"I believe you," I finally tell her. "But Tio Bruno doesn't know where we are. How will he find us?"

She lifts her pant leg. "He fitted me with a tracker. If

he realizes that I'm gone soon enough, he might already be on his way." She grips my shoulder. "I will do whatever I can to make sure our father doesn't get his hands on us. I just have to look like I'm playing along. The Kalku track my movements."

"What? How?"

"Bruno's not the only one who fitted me with a tracker." She taps a spot behind her ear. "Máximo implanted mine. He knows where I'm at. If we don't move toward the harbor, he'll send the Kalku to speed things along. Trust me, we don't want that."

"So we have to go towards the harbor, in the direction of Máximo's island. We have to move slow enough that Tio Bruno can catch up and intervene, and hopefully get us back to the village safely. But we have to move at a decent enough pace so the Kalku don't feel the need to step in and make us go faster. Did I get that right?"

Tavita's smile slides across her face without a hiccup, as if she is the kind of person who can find ease anywhere she lands, even in a scummy gas station bathroom. "Picture perfect, sis."

She's so easy to be with, careful with me, yet confident that we will be friends.

"You're taking care of me," I comment, emotion jerking in my chest.

Tavita softens. "Of course I am. I'm sorry you're not used to that. The way you handed Bruno's ass to him on the phone that one time, it's clear you're used to handling things by yourself." She tsks me gently. "No more. We have each other now. I'm the older sibling, so I get to set the tone. This is how I want us to be." Tavita winks at me. "You can take care of me when I'm hanging onto the toilet next time."

"Deal," I snigger, trying my best to catch up to her swagger. I really do like her.

I close my eyes. I can't believe it's come to hoping Tio Bruno shows up. Normally, I can't stand the man.

I do what I can to reach out to my new sister. "That must've been so frightening for you, not to be able to control your own body."

Tavita shakes her head, tears pricking her eyes without falling. "It's not just that. It's that I don't know who Máximo sacrificed! If it was Santiago, I'll never forgive myself."

Though I'm hanging onto a public toilet, I lift my head enough to give her what I hope is a bolstering look. "We'll find him. If it happens again that Máximo controls you, what would you like me to do?"

"Knock me out! Please, Adelita. Knock me out. He's evil, our father. Máximo wanted me to be rescued from his island, so when the soldiers came, he practically giftwrapped me for them. He wanted me taken into their village, so I could be an insider working for him. Why do you think I didn't speak and I didn't mind being locked away? I was trying to get everyone to shut up around me!"

She keeps rubbing circles on my back, kneeling beside me while we wait for the poison to attach itself to the new bites of the burrito, and then projectile out of my body.

"I'm the leak," Tavita admits woefully. "Though I didn't mean to be. When whichever one of you called Bruno first, they told him you were headed to the curse tree. Máximo heard that because Bruno was in the room with me when he got that call! Máximo sent the Kalku to take you when you visited Santos' curse tree."

"Are you serious?"

Tavita nods gravely. "Máximo wants us on the island with him. He wanted me because I can walk through walls. He wants you because you're strong."

I blink at her, stilling through the unbridled confession. "You... what?"

Her neck shrinks, and her eyes dart around the gas station bathroom, though we're the only ones here. "I can walk through walls if I concentrate hard enough."

I balk at her. "Are you serious? How?"

"The same way you can lift a car. I just can."

"I can't lift a car," I counter, though admittedly, that's only because I've never tried.

Her eyebrow raises, drawing out an unexpected snigger from me. I'm so out of sorts, I can't believe anything is funny right now.

"How do you think I got the clothes you're wearing? I don't have any money."

I glance down at the yoga pants and hoodie she procured for me on one of our stops.

"Santiago told me about your blessing—that you would only be as strong as you are gentle. I'm betting you can lift a car, no problem." She smooths a few loose hairs back from my face. "Santiago did that to me, too. Mine is a little different. I can only pass through if my intentions are good." She waves her hand back and forth and rolls her eyes. "He said it more poetically than that, but you get it." Her mouth tightens. "I guess when my brain was overridden by Father last night, I still had no evil intentions; those still belong to Father. I'm just the body that carries it out. So I was still able to walk through walls."

I take a few seconds to let that sink in.

Tavita rubs my back. "It's Santiago's way of limiting Máximo the only way anyone can. He can't undo our genetics, but he can put a hedge around our abilities, ensuring we don't turn out as power-hungry and manipulative as our father."

It's too much. I can't remain calm any longer. I'm dehydrated and exhausted. I'm kneeling on a rest area bathroom floor, bracing myself for my next wave of sick. My lower lip quivers, and I know I'm done, as far as meta conversations go. "I miss my mom!" I sob, unable to rein in my heartbreak. "I want to go home, but I don't even know where that is anymore."

My tears become hers. Maybe it's because we're sisters, maybe it's because we're in the same sinking ship, or maybe it's because she's empathetic. "I know, Sis. I feel you. My mom's been gone for two years, and I miss her every day. She'd know how to fix this."

My chin lifts. "Two years? When did she pass? How?"

"Car accident." Her throat scrapes raw. "I was taking her to the movies. It's our monthly girl date. We were hit from the side by the Kalku. She died on the spot, and I was taken by one of Father's goons."

"When? What month? What day?"

I'm cruel for making her talk about it in greater detail, but I have to know.

"May." Tavita swallows hard. "May 20th."

Panic surges through my body. "They did the same to me. Must've been them. Same month. Same year.

Same day. Bus crash. I was the only survivor because Santiago pulled me from the crash. That's when he blessed me, so I'd only be as strong as I was gentle."

"You're lucky," she says drily, though neither of us has been granted a stroke of fortune from where I sit. "Santiago told Máximo you beat him something horrible, but really he let you go. The Kalku who murdered my mother and abducted me weren't as merciful. Once Father had me, he turned his focus from capturing you to seeing if I could be his ticket to freedom instead." She flinches as the memory of her time on the island plagues her features. "All I can say is that I'm sorry I wasn't the tool Father needed, only because it forced his attention your way. When he wants something, he will not stop until he has it. Everyone and everything you love, he strips away. I wouldn't get attached to anyone in your life, if I were you. Máximo will tear it from you and crush it before your eyes just to amuse himself."

She's quiet a few beats while it sinks in that yes, in fact, I was lucky. Santiago could have been sent for her instead, and the Kalku could have been sent for me. Then I would have been the one to have been taken to live with a megalomaniac the day of my college graduation.

I can see the weathered look about her. Though she doesn't appear to be all that old, there's a sadness to her eyes that gives her a wizened, thoughtful countenance. I don't question that she has been through much, yet has found the determination to remain unburied.

Tavita tears off half a dozen squares of toilet paper and dabs at my mouth. "As soon as you're well enough to move, we have to keep going. If Father suspects I've defected, he'll send the Kalku for us."

My stomach heaves, and I know talking time is over. The burrito rockets out of me, hopefully with the last of the poison, while Tavita rubs slow circles across my back.

My mother was killed not by some ill-fated bus accident, but by a carefully planned attack by the Kalku.

I love my mother, and Máximo took her from me.

Vengeance curdles in my gut, sloshing through me as I vomit out the last of the poison my father gave me.

Just when I think my life cannot get any worse, the door bursts open and a slew of men in camo shirts flood my view, announcing that our time in hiding has come to an end.

6

THE CAVE OF THE KALKU
ADELITA

The Kalku don't understand that vomit is gross, nor do they care when my sick spills all the way down one of their backs. The chunks wet my captor's shirt so much that it sticks to his back, yet still, he marches on. They didn't blink an eye when I vomited in the backseat of their car, either. Or when the bulk of it landed in one of my captor's laps.

Tavita is unconscious. The blow to the head they gave her still makes me cringe. They didn't bother wounding me when they found us—the perks of being too weak to do more than lift my head.

The night does nothing to ease my worry. We're being taken somewhere that I don't know. I'm so turned around that I can't even sense the cardinal direction in which we're headed.

It's been hours that I keep drifting in and out of consciousness. I'm too dehydrated and weak. I've begged for water, but they haven't said a word to me.

I wonder if they're not allowed to speak to women, or if it's all prisoners they ignore.

These are goons, not the cave slaves, as Santos and Santiago were. And they aren't the Father of their clan, because they all wear their hair in long dreadlock-like braids. I remember Santos telling me something about the father of the clan being bald.

I wonder if this is the same Kalku clan that kidnapped Rafael.

Anger burns in my chest, though I'm too weak to maintain it for more than a minute at a time.

My eyes drift shut, even as I'm being carried so degradingly over this man's shoulder.

When I awake again, we're not in the car. We're high up—far too high up. I can feel pressure in my ears. I take in the craggy top of a cave, and realize I'm the one place a woman should never be if she wants to live.

I'm in the cave of the Kalku.

My heart is weak, but the staccato rhythm still makes an appearance, alerting the rest of my adrenal system that it's going to be all hands on deck.

The Kalku only bring women to their caves for ritual sacrifices. I remember the horrifying stories the guys used to tell me. They throw the women into a pit and leave her there for three days. By then she's so frightened that her heart is pounding. That's when the sacrifice is at its freshest. They cut out the woman's heart and throw it into a pot of boiling water, making a broth for the warriors. Whatever qualities the woman has, they believe they will get these things if they drink her heart stew.

Please don't let them throw me in a pit. If they do that, it's all over for me.

I turn my head to the side, trying to make out the shifting shapes in the moonlight near the mouth of the cave. When my vision comes into focus, all I see is my sleeping sister with a man bent beside her. His hair is shaggy and unbraided—a cave slave. He has a syringe of something that he pokes into Tavita's arm.

I open my mouth to scream at him to leave her alone, but nothing more than a pathetic croak comes out.

A bald man turns my head to the other side, filling my vision with a greedy gleam in his eyes. "Máximo will be pleased. He was hoping we would find one of his daughters. To return a second daughter to him? We will be greatly rewarded."

They won't put me in the pit, then. They plan to save me for Máximo. That shouldn't be a relief, given the monster I've been told Máximo is, but a gust of elation escapes me all the same.

"One can talk through walls," the leader says to the cave slave. "Best lower her down before she comes to and gives us the slip." Then he looks at me. "Are you the strong one, or the one who can walk through walls?"

Before I can even think to answer, he slaps me hard across the face.

My vision swims, my cheek smarting horribly. I want to ask him what that was for, but he's examining me. "Probably not the strong one, or you would've fought back." He stands, clicking his fingers to one of his soldiers. "Get her into the dark. Quick, now. Don't bother with the needle on this one. She won't be able to overpower us."

He thinks I'm Tavita.

Before I can tell him off, I'm scooped up and taken further into the cave. They don't use lanterns, which makes me wonder if they can see in the dark. I can't make out a thing as the darkness closes in around me like a tomb.

I have to get out of here. Yet even as I try to push the man away, I'm embarrassed by my futile attempt. I'm no more useful than a fly. I'm too dehydrated for tears to prick my eyes, but my heart shudders all the same. Have

I lost my strength because I've lost my gentleness? Have I changed so much that I can barely lift my own arm?

So lost in my existential crisis am I that I scarcely register my body being lowered into a hammock of sorts. It's a long strip of cloth that cradles me as it lifts and tightens, though not uncomfortably.

Then there's an ominous creak of a pulley overhead. The hammock swings out, and then lowers past the level of the floor on which I was just laid.

Down, down, down I go.

I panic, grasping at the rope to pull myself up. But just as I could barely lift my arm, I cannot heft myself up using the rope. The man controlling the pulley says nothing as he lowers me well past several stories. He keeps up the steady pace, even as I shout up to him, begging him to stop. "I don't understand! I don't... You can't put me in the pit! No! Let me out! Let me out!"

The moment I hit the bottom of the pit, he cuts the rope and slides something over the opening, sealing me inside with my terror.

7

COLD CAVE
ADELITA

I've lost track of the hours, whether they're actually minutes or whole days. I'm so dehydrated that I spend most of my time drifting in and out of consciousness. Sometime during the night, they lowered Tavita into the pit with me. Whatever the cave slave gave her knocked her out, and she still hasn't woken up.

It's freezing down here, so much that Tavita is icy to the touch. Though I'm just as cold, I'm fairly certain I'm too dehydrated to last much longer. There's no reason for both of us to die. I peel my hoodie over my head, groaning at the effort of the simple task. My muscles are locking down, protesting the slightest movement. I thread my sister's arms through the sweater and tug it carefully over her supine form.

The two hammocks are next. They're the only other things down here. The thin material isn't exactly insulating, but I'll take what I can get. I wrap up my sister as best I can, pulling the hood over her head and tucking in her hair. I weave her hands into the pouch in front, doing what I can to keep every part of her as warm as possible.

I might not have a chance at making it out, but Tavita will, so help me. I will not let my sister die in this pit.

Though I can't make anything better, I reach for my mother's memory in the dark, lulling Tavita with the song that centers me when I am out of sorts. My voice cracks across the syllables, and is poorly out of tune, but the love is there. It serves to warm us both, as much as words are able.

"SLEEP, BABY, SLEEP.
Dream, baby, dream.
Love, baby, love.
My baby, mine."

"MAMA," TAVITA COOS, BUT REMAINS MOSTLY unconscious. She's stirred a few times, but hasn't come fully back to herself. I wonder what sort of sedative they gave her.

The nightgown was beautiful when I first put it on. That seems like a thousand years ago. It's pale pink, strappy, short and low-cut. It's the sexiest thing I've ever worn to bed with two men. Now that it's paired with yoga pants, and serves as my source of warmth, I wish I'd gone to bed in a wool jacket instead.

My only silver lining is that I seem to have thrown up all the poison, so that's a bonus. I guess the other silver lining is that they didn't discover Tavita's tracker around her ankle.

I lay down beside my sister, curling up to her so we're not drifting in the dark. Her body anchors mine, so it doesn't feel quite so hollow. Everything is frightening, including the deafening silence.

I want to protect her—this woman I barely know. She's the older sibling, but still, I fawn over her hair, making sure there are no pesky fly-aways tickling her forehead. I don't know all she's been through. I barely know a sliver of her pain, but she remained in control of herself, planning her silence to keep Cáceres safe from Máximo's eavesdropping. Even though we were a bunch of strangers to her, she did all she could to keep him from infiltrating our tribe.

Our tribe.

That sure sneaked up on me.

"Rafi," I rasp in the dark. "Rafi, don't stop looking for me."

"Santos," I whisper, as if he can hear me. "Santos, I would free the cave slaves if I could get out of this place! Santos, I'm sorry."

I don't want to call for Cruz, mainly because saying his name will make the whole thing real. If I call for Cruz and he doesn't come, then I truly am stuck in the bottom of a pit.

If I call for Cruz and he doesn't save the day?

It's up to me to save us. I know this, but I can't stand without pain in my bones.

I cannot save my last scrap of family.

Finally, I cry his name because it's my last hope. "Cruz," I whimper. "Cruz, I need help."

Last of all, I call for my mother, who never comes for me anymore when I'm afraid.

I close my eyes, holding my sister and wishing I could save us.

Part of my soul breaks off and withers at the silence that greets me. If Santos could save me, there's nothing that would hold him back. If Cruz could track me down, he would already have done so. He can find me anywhere.

I stare into the void, welcoming death that will surely come for me first.

Minutes turn into hours, or maybe it's merely seconds that pass before a disturbance rumbles overhead. I haven't been able to hear anything, isolated as we are, but there's a muffled... *something* that draws my attention.

"Tavita?" I try to rouse my sister, but she's still unconscious.

I don't understand what's happening, but I'm not willing to take any chances. With my last burst of energy, I roll Tavita toward the side of the pit, so if they hurl something down at us, there's less of a chance it could pierce her.

Once she's pressed to the wall, I curl my arms around my sister, shielding her with my body while I wait for the Kalku to come for our hearts.

8

HEART-STOPPING BEAUTIES
BRUNO

"The only men worth taking are the cave slaves. Everyone else dies," I order, though my men already know as much. It's the same drill we always follow when we infiltrate one of their caves. This time, however, the stakes are higher. It's not some random prisoner we're hoping to liberate. It's... It's Cruz's future bride and the potential mother to the heir of the family bloodline.

Sure, that's why I've been driving like a maniac and brought along my no-nonsense weapons, along with some of my cruelest fighters. For Adelita.

As we scale the side of the mountain with our shields up to fend off their weapons that shower down on us, I know without a doubt I'm pushing myself to my limits for Tavita alone. She is the reason I'm leading the charge, instead of falling back to let the less-seasoned soldiers take the first line of defense.

There's a connection I feel to this woman who wouldn't tell me even her name. There was an understanding in her eyes.

She wanted to be near me.

No woman ever wants to be near me. My own nieces skitter away when I come to the table. Yet Tavita rested her head on my chest, as if she knew I would transform myself into a pillow, if that's what she needed. I would be her soft spot to rest.

I don't care that I sound like a sap. I've been traveling all day and night. Now that dawn is here, I will tear apart every man who took her where she didn't want to go. I wanted to put her in a hut in the village, but when she didn't want to be moved from the cell, I respected her wishes. When she indicated she wanted to be locked inside, I did as she asked. These barbarians deserve to have their throats cut out for taking her here, no doubt against her wishes.

At least, I hope she didn't wish for this. She can't be in league with the Kalku.

And if she is, I need to see the evidence with my own two eyes. When her ankle tracker led us here, hope began to fill me. The Kalku don't allow women into their caves, unless they're to be sacrificed. The mission to rescue Adelita from Tavita quickly changed to a vendetta to slaughter the Kalku who somehow captured both Adelita and Tavita.

It's the only explanation I'll accept.

I move faster up the mountain than I thought possible. The sting of the morning air keeps my muscles moving, my fingertips gripping the gray rock that seems never ending in its skyward pursuit. The ache in my joints is a passive cry I cannot pay attention to now. I'm racing toward Tavita because *I* want to be the one to rescue her. I don't want one of my men to see her compromised, if that is the state in which we find her.

Whenever I brought her meal, she would finish quickly without leaving a crumb. But when I would offer to go get her more, she wouldn't accept it. That told me she didn't have enough food on the island, but she's too prideful to ask for more.

I started bringing her double portions, which turned out to be partly selfish, because I love watching a woman eat who's not afraid of food.

Tavita won't want the men to see her deteriorated— whatever that might mean. I will protect her pride, because it is precious to her.

The second my hand reaches the ledge of the precipice, there's no chance of me slowing. Instead of adhering to my own instructions when I trained the soldiers time and time again to be cautious when you reach the opening of a cave, I forego caution and throw my lower half up and over the edge. Then I pump my biceps enough to hoist myself the rest of the way over.

I don't care that they're armed and ready for us. As they snarl, readying to take me out, there is no doubt in my mind that their hearts will stop beating this very day.

I rip my short sword from my sheath the second I find my footing, slicing across a Kalku's abdomen without polish. Each move is connected to the next. I don't stop at the slice, but follow the arc until it meets the face of the man beside him, fileting his cheek open without mercy.

I'm a man unhinged as I spin and slice again, carving across a warrior's throat so quickly that I'm gone from his presence before the blood has a chance to spurt out across my leather breastplate.

I lose count after that. The only thing my mind registers is my men versus theirs. It's the only distinction I need.

I don't waste time with threats or grunts of frustration or heroism. I'm here to take back the women they stole from my barracks. My home.

I refuse to believe Tavita left on her own. I cannot comprehend it, even though it's the only thing that makes sense. My gut rarely lies to me. Even though all the evidence points to Tavita escaping my barracks, then drugging the three and kidnapping Adelita, I cannot believe it. I need to look into Tavita's eyes and see the truth for myself.

Until she tells me she is just as wicked as her father, I will not stop fighting to find her.

Even though she was the only one in the room who heard where Cruz was headed when they went to the curse tree, and were subsequently ambushed by the Kalku, I still can't bring myself to admit I was wrong about her.

When Tavita's tracker showed up in the cave of the Kalku, I knew she could not be against us. They had done this. They had drugged the three and taken Adelita, along with my Tavita.

That's the only explanation I'll accept. Over and over, I repeat this to myself, this logic on a loop. Even while I slaughter the savages in this cave, my mind is solely on Tavita.

It's only when one of my men shouts for me to stop that I realize I'm inches from gutting a cave slave.

They never fight us, even when they've been raised with the Kalku from birth. No matter how they've been conditioned to assume torture is necessary and superstition is the only way of life, some surviving goodness lingers, letting them know that this way is wrong.

Or maybe they've been so mistreated by their superiors that they're more than happy to lay down their weapons. They no doubt understand that their brethren would sooner kill them than let their slaves be liberated.

I release the man with no shirt, ratty shorts and shaggy hair, who immediately drops to his knees and laces his hands behind his neck in surrender. One of my men zip ties his hands to the base of his back. Even though it's not ideal for traveling down a mountainside, this is how it's done.

I look around, hoping for another offender to kill. I don't want to be angry with Tavita for betraying my trust. I don't want to believe it's possible, so I'm determined to take my anger out on my enemy until none of them are left standing.

Even my soldiers give me a wide berth while my chest heaves.

"Has anyone killed the father?" I bellow. "Where is the leader of this clan?"

It's procedure to keep the father alive for last, in case any information needs to be extracted.

One of my soldiers already has him secured and on his knees. "Here, Commander."

No matter how old and frail they always look, the fathers of the differing Kalku clans are all the same brand of evil. They abduct women and tear out their hearts. They cause chaos for our tribes. They are in league with Máximo, which is crime enough to deserve a swift death.

This leader is no different. "Do what you will," he says to me, his rounded face unapologetic. Though his steadiness is admirable, it will not save him.

"Where are the women?"

The bald cave father's chin lifts. "They are at the base of the mountain on the east side."

I know he is lying, so I slice across his abdomen, which is a truly painful way to bleed out. "Where are the women?"

He grits his teeth through a tearless sob of agony. "They belong to the Kalku, so they will die with our bodies!"

I nod to the soldier who secured him, and my man slits the father's throat. He is of no use to us any longer.

The voice of the cave slave hits my ears as the wind picks up. "Father was lying. The women are in the pit. It's at the very back of the cave."

He doesn't dare ask to get up and show me, which I appreciate.

"There's a covering over it. I don't think it was moved, but it might've been shifted about in the fray. If you can't see in the dark, you'll fall right into the hole, so make sure you watch your steps."

"Very good." I reach down and place my hand atop his head, noting his flinch. "You are safe now. What is your name?"

"David."

"Stay right where you are, David. If you keep your head about you, we'll get you out of here without incident. Are you hurt?"

"No, sir. Are they... Are they all dead?"

There's hope in his voice.

He wasn't brought here as a child. Those ones want to be liberated, but they're usually too afraid to leave the cave, since they've not been allowed out of it their whole lives.

"They are. How long have you been here, David?"

"A year. Please, help me get home!"

"Absolutely. Let us fish out the women, and we'll get you out of here."

"There's a pulley system," he informs me. "You can use it to get them out."

"That's good, David." I stand and steel myself for the rescue. "Search the cave!" I shout to my soldiers.

They are tired, but they don't act like it. They rush to obey, high from the thrill of our victory. Usually quests to take down a faction of the Kalku are carefully plotted for weeks, with several ups and downs along the way. This siege has to be some sort of record.

Flashlights come out and three of my soldiers lead the way toward the back of the cave. They are careful with their steps, but even so, one of them slips on the covering and nearly falls through.

"Steady!" his compatriot chides, ripping him away from the edge.

I trot toward them and peer down into the pit. No part of me expected them to be this far down. Is that three stories? Four? "How did…"

I shake my head and cast around for the pulley. The thing looks ancient, though the iron frame appears steady enough for even my weight.

I hope.

When one of my men steps toward the cloth seat that sort of looks like a mini hammock or a swing and attaches it to the hook on the pulley, my chest makes this odd rumbling noise. "I'll be going down."

The soldier steps back, though it's clear he doesn't expect me to do more of the grunt work. I already demolished most of the Kalku in this cave. I'll not be robbed of Tavita's face. I need to see if she was lying this whole time. I need to know if my gut could be so easily tricked by a beautiful face.

Two of my men work the pulley, moving the lever slowly so I don't descend too quickly, or lose my balance on the tiny swing and fall to my death. I'm very aware of how much I trust my soldiers to get me back out of here. If they decided they wanted to be done with my unbending rule, they could easily leave me in the pit to rot until my body gave up hope. But they are good soldiers, so I don't dwell on that horror for more than a few fleeting seconds.

The dark is oppressive, even though I've got a flashlight in my fist, along with a few shining down on me from above. The walls are narrow—maybe six feet or so across. The smell of mold greets me, along with wet rock.

When my feet hit the ground, I cannot school my features against the horror that hits me. Sure, Adelita isn't my favorite person, but she is my nephew's favorite person. To see the future first lady of our tribe lifeless on the ground with a shiner? It's too much for my rage to handle gracefully. Her lips are cracked, she looks fragile, and when she sees me, I'm not sure she recognizes my face.

"Cruz?" she rasps.

It's then I realize I'm shining the light in her face, and she's been in complete darkness for who knows how long. I move the beam to the body beside hers, noting the lack of movement.

I swallow hard as I reach for Adelita, knowing the pecking order demands I rescue the future tribe ruler's future wife first, even though my heart screams for Tavita.

I need answers. I need to know if it was all a lie.

But when I reach for Adelita, she flinches away. "No. Take Tavita up first. Save my sister. She... you have to save her!"

"Did she abduct you?" I ask. Even though Adelita is barely alive, I have to know.

"Máximo," Adelita replies, her voice a pained rasp. "Máximo controls her body. Get her out, but bind her hands, so Máximo can't make her hurt anyone. Hurry." Though I can tell she means to speak with urgency, Adelita's eyes close as her voice fades.

I take that as a directive and grant myself the gift of cradling Tavita in my arms. She's out cold, but her pulse is steady. Because no one is looking, I bury my nose in her cheek, holding her as close as I want.

I knew she hadn't betrayed us.

I sit back in the cloth swing with Tavita unconscious across my lap. I leave the flashlight with Adelita and tug on the rope. "Take us up," I call, and they do.

I curse every slight jerk as we glide upwards. I don't know if Tavita is injured. I don't know what they've done to her. I don't know why she didn't wake when she heard my voice. Fear grips me when I realize the rescue isn't nearly over. Neither of these women are out of the woods yet.

When my head emerges from the hole, I reluctantly hand off Tavita to one of my married soldiers. I select carefully, because Tavita is too beautiful not to fall in love with at first glance. "Bind her hands, but don't hurt her. Adelita said she was being controlled by Máximo. When she comes to, he might try to control her again, so make sure she can't attack us or herself."

"Yes, Commander."

Though he says it easily, I worry he'll do the bindings too tight. "I don't want to see marks on her wrists."

He nods to me, though I can tell he's perplexed as to how to zip tie a person and not leave marks, while also securing them from escape.

Whatever. His problem to solve, not mine.

I loathe the second descent because it goes so slowly. I want to get out of here already and get Tavita to a healer. Adelita looks like she needs one, too.

By the time my feet touch down, Adelita is completely out. Though her curves should add some weight to her, she's a feather in my arms, lifeless as she is. When I search for her pulse, my own plummets when I don't feel it at first.

I lay her back down, frightened as flashes of Cruz's impending grief flood my mind if I don't bring back his girlfriend alive. Quickly, I open her mouth and fish my finger in her mouth to see if anything is blocking her airway.

Her tongue is dry. The entire cavern of her throat is parched beyond reason. "I need a canteen! She needs water now!" I call up. Still, I don't feel her pulse, so I steel myself and start a round of CPR, pumping down on her sternum with what I hope is the right amount of force. She looks so fragile; I don't want to splinter her ribs.

Before I can put my mouth to hers, a canteen bangs to the ground beside me, and then bounces to knock my side. I snatch it up and tilt Adelita's upper half. The water that sloshes into her mouth trickles down her throat, but nothing constricts.

I massage her throat, coaxing it to life as best I can, hoping that I haven't come too late. I should have brought Adelita up first, but I let my affections cloud my judgment. Adelita is the only one who can chase away La Sayona. Cruz needs her. Without Adelita, my brother's bloodline will die out. He is next to rule. Roberto is still more than a decade out from being able to take the leading spot. It will go to Cruz, who, without Adelita, will not last long, nor will he settle down.

I cannot let this woman die.

I splash a few more glugs into her mouth, and then

lie her back down. The rhythm I pump into her chest remains steady, even when I fear my own heart might give out from the stress of it all.

A sob of relief escapes me when Adelita's chest finally moves on its own.

My shoulders deflate. "Good! That's good, Adelita." I tilt her upper half in the crook of my arm and poise the canteen to her lips. "Another drink now. Easy, kiddo."

And that's exactly what she is to me. The irritating girl next door who's always right, and who ends up dating your family member so you can never be rid of her.

I smile down at Adelita as she opens her eyes. I don't have to like her. Maybe that's our thing. She goads me, and I loathe her for it. So long as she's good to Cruz, Rafi and Santos, that's all I care about.

I have to get her back to the village so a healer can look at her. "Your heart stopped," I murmur, tipping the canteen to her lips after she takes a few breaths. "Drink slowly."

The slip of a nightgown she's wearing over stretchy black pants does nothing to cover her breasts. It's freezing down here. I lay her back down and tear my sweaty and bloodstained t-shirt over my head, so one of her boobs doesn't accidentally pop out.

"I've got a blanket in the car," I offer when she shivers.

"Tavita?" she rasps.

"Shh. Your throat isn't ready for conversation. A few more sips. Tavita is safe up there with my soldiers. I told them to do as you said. No one's going to hurt her."

Adelita gusts out her relief.

I gather Adelita into my arms and situate myself on the seat, pressing the canteen to her chest.

I jerk on the rope. "Hurry! Cruz's bride needs a healer."

She is slight in my arms, and weak as a newborn. This vixen who sparred with me over dinner can't even say my name now.

Righteous rage kindles behind my ribs. This rescue may be over, but my fight with Máximo is just beginning.

9

SISTERS AND SCALPELS
BRUNO

I'm careful with Adelita as I carry her into the morning sun. She's been in pitch black for too long, so the brightness will take some time for her eyes to adjust to. I tell my soldier to bring Tavita to the cave's mouth, too. I don't like it when I can't see her.

"Clean up the bodies," I instruct my men. "Take their weapons and put them in a pile, then throw their bodies into the pit. You know the drill. Tavita shouldn't have to see a bunch of dead carcasses when she wakes." Then, to cover over my obvious tell, I add, "Adelita, either."

My soldiers work quickly to clean up the wreckage. Their hustle quells my worry that I'm getting old, and that one day, I might be irrelevant to them.

I keep checking to make sure Adelita's heart is still beating. The rhythm is slow and weak, but it's there. Her body is still a noodle, so I sit near the entrance of the cave and situate her across my lap. It's intimate in a way that I know we both loathe, but it's necessary. Her head flops in the crook of my arm, but I keep it steady as I tip the canteen to her lips again. Each gulp revives her a modest amount, but I know from experience that this sort of thing needs to happen slowly.

"Tracking device," Adelita tells me during one of her rare moments of lucidity.

"That's right. That's how I found you. I put a tracker on Tavita's ankle when she was first brought to us."

"No," she protests, "Máximo. He put a tracker in her. Behind her ear. It controls her. He can listen to our conversations using that." She steadies herself for a few breaths, because the effort of speaking is too much. "You have to take it out, or he will always come for her."

Shock hits my system. "What?!" I call for Guillermo, who's served in my army for two decades. "I need you to hold the princess for a minute while I check on Tavita. Careful with her. Small sips of water every so often. Her heart stopped down in the pit. Make sure not to jostle her too much."

Guillermo takes each assignment I give him seriously, which is why I trust him with the most important things. He cradles Adelita as if she was his own child, which, given how frail she looks, suits the image perfectly.

I kneel beside Tavita's unconscious form, checking her pulse because I need to know it's there. Her heart is strong and steady, so my hand moves to the space behind her ear. When I don't find anything unusual, I turn Tavita to her other side, wondering if Adelita's warning was the musings of a mind driven to madness.

But when my fingers skitter over a lump, my entire body freezes. How I didn't notice something so obvious before is beyond me. There it is, an inch-long thin tube beside a line of scar tissue. She was cut into so this device could be sewn in.

I need to get her to the village, to a healer, but I can't alert Máximo by saying too much. Who knows what he could do to her through this device. Is there a lethal chemical inside for when his daughter defects? All I know is that it needs to come out now.

I cast around to my soldiers, rating their field medical experience as a collective low. They can bandage up a wound in a pinch, sure, but they're not healers who have trained with a scalpel.

When my eyes fall on David, still on his belly with his hands bound at the base of his back, he meets my gaze with purpose. "I can help her."

It's a promise I don't want to believe, but there's no other option. "What do you know about it?"

David jerks his head, indicating he needs to talk to me in private.

I stalk over to the cave slave, my knife drawn.

David's voice is just above a whisper. "The Kalku talked about her tracker. Máximo put that in her to mark her movements. He can control her actions with it, too, but he has to sacrifice a person to conjure up the magic to push her to do his will. He can hear through it, too. Máximo cannot hear her in the night, but it's daytime now, so be careful with your words." He eyes Tavita across the way. "That thing needs to come out now. I don't know what else it might be able to do to her."

My eyes close as understanding hits me. "So that's why she refused to speak for so long. She didn't want Máximo to overhear anything."

"Smart girl. She was protecting you."

"She insisted she be locked in a cell alone well beyond the isolation time a rescue might need."

"Like I said, smart girl."

I close my eyes. "I'm guessing this will be hard to explain to a hospital."

David coughs a few times. "I was in my last year of medical school when the Kalku abducted me. I'm their healer in here. I'm not as qualified as an actual surgeon, but I can look at it, if you like."

He doesn't ask to be let up, or even to have his hands untied. He simply offers the information I need with no caveat.

I go with my gut, since it was right in trusting Tavita.

I dictate my actions to the soldiers as I cut the twenty-something man's bindings. "Don't try anything, alright? I'm trusting you. I have every intention of taking you to our village so you can get back on your feet."

David shakes his head. "I don't want to go anywhere but home. If you could drop me there, that's all I need."

I pause, taking in his request. "It's not protocol. You've been here for a year. That takes a toll on a person. You need rehabilitation." I help him sit up.

David rubs his wrists and then feathers his fingers through dark, shaggy hair. "I'll sign up for whatever rehab you like, but I need to go home. I have a wife and a son. I've been missing for a year. That's where I belong."

His eyes glisten, but tears don't fall. This man loves his family more than his own safety. I cannot begrudge him this concession. "Alright. We can do that. But we don't halfway rescue someone when they've been taken by the Kalku. I'll be sending someone to check on you every week for the next year, to make sure you're stable.

I don't want a destroyed wife and son on my hands because you didn't get proper help."

David hesitates, but then nods. "That's fair. All I can think of is getting home to them. Everything else is just words. But that makes sense. Thanks for caring about them enough to intervene. I'll make sure I'm there for the weekly check-ins."

His humility shocks sense into me. That's how a man should behave who loves his family. Focused on being with them, and willing to get help if he's not his best self for them.

David dictates his movements to me before he makes them, so no one spooks and attacks. "I'm getting my healer bag. It's got a scalpel. If anyone could start a fire so I can disinfect it, that would be much appreciated."

David goes about his business of prepping while one of my soldiers kindles a small fire. The bodies are nearly all in the pit, and I'm anxious to get moving. I don't like the haunted feel of the cave. Every time I go on one of these missions, the victory is marred by the lingering sinister vibe lurking in the air.

The weapons are piled in the corner while we wait for David to do a precursory examination of his newest patient. He's sweating, which doesn't bode well.

"Do you know what you're doing?"

He frowns up at me, and then moves away from Tavita, no doubt to keep Máximo from overhearing. "The most qualified surgeon on the planet wouldn't know what they were doing with this. I have no reference for this kind of technology. This whole organization is a mix a cavemen and technological geniuses, with little in between. I can tell you that I've studied several procedures similar to this—digging foreign subdermal objects from a person, but none of that was anything like this. I'm your only option, unless you want to take her to a hospital. They'll be more qualified and have better tools there, but the second Máximo catches wind she's trying to have the device taken out, he will act, and I don't know how deadly that action might be, or how immediate."

I scrub my hand over my face. "Alright. Then carry on."

I've never felt more conflicted. I'm either letting this man save her life, or I'm watching while he kills her.

David pauses before he turns around. "You might want to not be near the scene."

"How's that?"

"I'm about to cut your girlfriend open, and I can't give her more sedative. They had me give her the maximum dose already. They wanted her out for as long as possible, and I'm sure we're nearing the end of it. But

I don't feel comfortable risking her health for the sake of her pain. So I'm going to have to do this without anything to numb the area. If she screams through it, I'll need one of your men to hold her steady so I don't make things worse."

Agony tears at my gut as I move to her side. "I can hold her down." More like, I can't stomach watching a man hold her down. At least this way, I can loathe myself properly.

If she dies, this will be my fault. I'm letting this happen. I'm holding her down while it happens.

The cold breeze smacks my bare chest as I roll Tavita onto her side. I have nothing with which to tie back her hair, so I wind the black tresses in my fist, curling them around my hand to further help keep her head from thrashing about if this thing goes south.

I cannot breathe when David makes his first incision.

When Tavita's eyes open and her screams fill the cave, I know I will never forgive myself for her pain. I can only hope she makes it through the procedure, so she can live to curse me to my grave.

10

TAVITA'S WISH
BRUNO

I am not accustomed to sitting in an emergency room's cubicle, waiting patiently. Our healers in the village usually handle everything, but given that Adelita's heart stopped beating, I didn't think it wise to chance a day-long drive to get us to the village.

And even though Tavita made it through the procedure of having Máximo's tracking device removed, I still wanted to make sure her wound was properly cleaned and whatnot.

At least I'm not splitting my time between two rooms anymore. Tavita's checkup went smoothly, so I'm less anxious overall. I texted my soldiers who were dropping David at his home the message of her positive state, just so David had an update on his patient.

Even though Tavita is sitting right beside me in these ridiculously uncomfortable plastic chairs, I can't for the life of me figure out what to say to her.

I should interrogate her, being that she unwittingly abducted Adelita and drugged the three of them. I should get to the bottom of how she thought it was a good idea to tell me nothing, when I could have helped her back in the village.

But when my mouth finally opens, all that tumbles out is a graceless, "You scared me half to death."

Tavita snorts in my direction. "Only half? I must've been off my game. Usually when I'm being controlled by a monster, I go full-force."

"I could have helped you. Why didn't you tell me?"

She shakes her head, though I can tell that slight movement gives her stitches pause. "Father told me he would murder anyone who found out. I've seen his lust for gore. I had no reason to believe he wouldn't tear you apart if I told you the truth."

"But you told Adelita."

Her eyes fix on her unconscious sister, who's still lying in the bed, hooked to tubes and monitors. "I knew he wouldn't kill her. Father needs her alive. She's the only person he's afraid to hurt." Her gaze combs over Adelita, as if checking her visually for damage from a distance. "Might as well lay all my cards out on the table now." She sighs heavily, and I brace myself for whatever is about to come. "Máximo is wary of me because I can walk through walls. He doesn't trust what he can't control."

I throw my head back and bang it against the wall three times. "Is there no end to all the things I don't know about you?"

She casts me a wry smile. "Well, we haven't actually known each other all that long, and they weren't under the best of circumstances. I'm guessing there's a whole sea of things we don't know about each other yet." She keeps her eyes from me, fixing them again on Adelita. "But I'm here now, and I'm ready to talk." Her finger flits from her armrest over to mine, brushing the back of my hand with the smallest of touches.

She's touching me. We're not in the cell. She's got no trace of captivity to her, yet she's touching me. My stomach flips. If she keeps this up, I'll do whatever she asks.

Her voice is gentle when she says, "I'm not going anywhere, Bruno."

Relief loosens the stranglehold my ribs have had on my chest, and finally, I breathe. "I'm glad to hear that. Back to the cell, then, Blue Eyes?"

It still works. She still blushes at the nickname.

Her hand rests atop mine, like it's no big thing, her middle finger stroking a featherlight tickle over the top of my knuckle. As if women do this sort of tender touch to me all the time. "I was thinking about your offer to stay in one of the huts in the village. Would that still be possible? I might need your help finding a job and getting on my feet."

I shift in my seat. "First things first. Of course you can have a hut. I picked one out for you a week ago. But you don't need to work or get on your feet right away. We have an acclimation plan for rescues."

We don't, actually, but now we do. I'm coming up with it on the fly because now that I'm putting Tavita's face on the plan, I realize how unhelpful our help really is to refugees. We can do more than send her to a healer and turn her out of the village.

She has nowhere to go. If she returns to her home, the Kalku will hunt her down and take her straight back to Máximo. Cáceres shouldn't cling to its walls like this. We should be better than the bare minimum.

I clear my throat. "It's unreasonable to expect you can start a normal life right after being liberated from the Kalku. Two months of living in the rescue hut. Your food and lodging are paid for already. It's the perks of being part of a tribe. Then, when we think you're ready, we'll find you a job in the village if you'd like to stay in Cáceres, or we'll help set you up in the outside world, if that's what you want."

Please don't want to leave.

"I can stay in Cáceres?"

Another gust of relief breathes life into my bones. She reached out to me, so I go out on a limb with full honesty. "I'd prefer it."

Her fingers thread through mine atop my armrest. "Me, too. Does Cáceres have a physical therapy clinic?"

I shrug. "We have healers. They do all that stuff as much as they can."

"And let me guess, they're all afraid of you?"

It's my turn to snort. "Everyone's afraid of me. So yeah, I guess they are. Why do you ask?"

"Because I'm thinking you'll be my first patient. If I can make it so your knees don't bother you so much, can we ease up on the two-month restriction? I do best when I'm working. I don't like sitting around. Too much time with my thoughts isn't a good thing. I don't like thinking about the island. I'd rather have the distraction."

My lips purse. "There's nothing wrong with my knees, and you're not going to skirt the rules just because you're afraid to deal with all you went through. The two-month acclimation exists for a reason."

Sure it does. Because I invented it just now.

My thumb trails across hers. "I want you functional when you reenter society, not running around half on your game and half out of your mind."

Maybe that was harsh, but it's true. Well, all except for the bit about my knees being fine. That was an outright lie. But she doesn't need to know how much of an old man I am. I saw her file. She's thirty-two. I'm fifty. That's not a gap that's going to go away. Reminding her of my aches and pains is no way to show Tavita I'm capable of keeping up with her.

Tavita motions to my jaw. "You grit your teeth when you sit down and when you stand. Lie to me all you want, but you're going to be my first patient."

I can't keep this up. Maybe she thinks I'm only a couple years older, and that's why she's still touching my hand. "I'm fifty years old, Tavi. Knees do that at my age."

This is it. This is when she'll pull away. But honestly, how could she not already know I'm much older than her? I look every bit as old as I am, and then some, I'm sure.

She keeps her gaze fixed on Adelita. "You're beautiful, is what you are. And I'm a hundred years old, so you might have to slow it down for me."

She pauses for my chuckle, and the blush I can feel heating my cheeks. I can't remember the last time that happened.

Beautiful? Never in my entire life has anyone called me that.

Tavita thumbs my fingertips. "I don't mind the age gap. If it bothers you, well, then get over it."

Her moxie is just about the sexiest thing I've ever come across in my life. I love the look of laughter in her eyes and the sound of a tease on her lips.

"It doesn't bother me until you talk about my old knees," I admit, casting her a smile.

"I'm not going to talk about them. I'm going to rehabilitate them. And you're not going to be a stubborn mule about it."

"Is that so?" Fates, she's perfect. I love that she's not afraid of me. And no part of my being wants to remedy that detail.

"It's very much so." We sit in silence, watching Adelita breathe while the IV does what it's supposed to do, pumping her full of hydration and missing nutrients. When Tavita speaks again, her voice is quiet, contemplative, and without the teasing I very much love. "I wanted to talk to you, back when I was in the cell. I wanted to tell you everything."

I take a chance and press her knuckles to my lips, giving them a light kiss.

I can tell right away that was both the right choice and the wrong one. I am infinitely more addicted to her, now that I've had a taste. "I know you did." I didn't know, but I hoped. "Why don't you start now? Tell me everything. Tell me anything."

She blinks a few times. "I hardly know where to begin. My real life feels like it was so long ago."

I don't have to prod her to open up. Now that her tongue is loosed, I know the details of her life will come to me if I'm patient. All I have to do is give her the space to explore her own thoughts without pushing them to make sense right away.

"Adelita and I both lost our moms on the same day. The Kalku were behind it. But Santiago was sent to bring Adelita in, and a pack of human jackals were sent to fetch me. Santiago has a soul, so he let her go, blessed her, and was punished severely for it. Father stopped looking for her because he had me to focus on."

I take in her truth and mull on it for a moment. "You have every right to be upset about that. It could've been Adelita taken, and you could've been free for the past two years. It's unfair."

She turns her head toward me. "Just the opposite. It's good I was taken and Adelita was set free. She had two years to live her life without Father. I already lived free through my twenties. Every smile she has, every moment with her boyfriend she enjoys, none of that would exist if Máximo had stolen her instead of me. I would never want her to go through what I had to on the island. I don't know Adelita yet, but I want to. I always wanted to be a good sister. To have a good sister."

My throat is dry, rough with confusion that comes when people are too altruistic and unselfish to make sense. "Sounds like you got your wish there. Both of them. You're a very good sister not to resent her. And, well, I guess you could do worse than to have a sister like Adelita. She's annoyingly right all the time, and she talks back like she's not afraid of anything. But as far as sisters go, you'll do alright with her."

Another bout of silence fills the room.

When Tavita speaks again, her voice is no louder than a whisper. "Bruno?"

The sound of emotion choking her volume garners my full attention. "Yes, Blue Eyes? What is it?"

"Will I be safe in Cáceres?"

How I want to scoop her in my arms and dash her away from all of this. "On my honor. No one will hurt you if I'm around."

She nods and then leans her temple to my shoulder.

She doesn't say a word, but I can feel her trust as it seeps into my skin.

I like it here. I like it very much.

It's only when Tavita excuses herself to use the restroom twenty minutes later that either of us moves.

Adelita's eyes pop open, and she turns her chin toward me. "I can only pretend to be asleep for so long. Are you going to kiss my sister or what?"

11

WRESTLING
BRUNO

'm overly careful with the sisters as I drive them back to Cáceres. Even when Adelita insists we stop at the hospital where Rafi took Santos and Cruz to be treated for dehydration, I don't veer from our path. Máximo will be hunting for his lost treasure soon enough. I need to get as much protection around us as possible before that happens.

Every crack in the road, I try to avoid, because each noise of discomfort Adelita makes sets a firm frown on Tavita's pink lips.

I haven't kissed Tavita, mostly because I haven't kissed anyone in a very long time, and I'm psyching myself out about it. Also, she's been through a trauma. She doesn't need me sniffing around her so blatantly just yet.

So I'll sniff around her circuitously, setting her up in a hut that rests on a street where two of my soldiers live. I'll double the security around Cáceres. I'll make sure her hut has every available precaution set in place.

I hate that I feed her stupid food I have to order through a window. Though she doesn't strike me as the type to turn up her nose at drive-thru tacos, she deserves better than this slop.

Adelita can't eat more than a few bites before she begs off.

Tavita speaks to Adelita as if she's five. "Honey girl, you need to eat. I know your stomach is sensitive, but food matters."

Adelita frowns at the taco. "I don't think I can take another crumb. I'm serious. It's about to all come back up. I don't think sustenance does much good if I can't keep it down."

"Fair point. Okay. Let's give you a few minutes to digest, and we'll try again."

They're sitting together in the backseat. It's clear to me how very much Tavita has always wanted a sibling. She's braided Adelita's hair into a thick crown. She doesn't let Adelita hold the cup of water, but insists on pressing the straw to her sister's lips. Every need Adelita expresses, Tavita sees to it. It's sweet, watching her be all maternal.

And honestly, I regret signing Adelita out of the emergency room before the doctor gave her the all-clear. But they were talking about keeping her overnight, and there's no way I can protect the girls from Máximo in there. The best place for their safety is Cáceres, even if Adelita looks like she might faint before we get there.

Adelita laps up the affection, soaking in the female companionship I can tell she's been missing. The two fawn over each other like newborn kittens. It's strange to watch, but fascinating as I drive along on the highway.

José and I were never like that.

When I put in a call to Javier, there's no chance of keeping it quiet, stuck as we are in the same vehicle. "Javi, I need you to get a hut ready for Tavita." I list off two streets near my own that would be acceptable for her to reside. "I'm bringing home Tavita and Adelita now. We'll be there by nightfall."

The Bluetooth sends Javier's voice through the car. "Yes, Commander."

"She'll need new clothes. The kitchen needs to be stocked. Charge it to my account." I really wish I could have this conversation in private. "Ask Consuela to pick out bedsheets. I'm no good at that sort of thing. They need to be soft, okay? They're for Cruz's future bride's sister, so make sure she gets the best."

"I'll see to it. Are you certain you wouldn't like me to set her up in Don José's home?"

My eyes flick to Tavita, who grimaces and quickly shakes her head.

I nod in response. "I think she prefers to acclimate in private, rather than with an audience."

"Very good, Commander. I'll have a healer ready for her, as well."

"Good man." I end the call, though I know the tips of my ears are pink. Tavita doesn't need to know that I care if she has nice sheets. That's too personal for a woman I haven't even kissed.

Adelita is the one who has something to say, though. "Why did you call me that?"

I fiddle with the temperature control. "What? I didn't call you annoying. I only thought it."

Adelita mimes a sarcastic laugh. "Not that. You called me Cruz's future bride. That's nothing like the truth."

My gaze flicks to the rearview mirror. "It's what everyone calls you. I don't remember when it started. It matters that people pay you the proper respect." When Adelita seems more offended than enlightened, I elaborate. "Look, like it or not, you weren't born in Cáceres. Everyone in the village is wary of outsiders. The walls keep new people out and old ideals in. It's going to be a long road to get the tribe to accept you. Calling you what you are—Cruz's future bride—shuts the more bigoted people up."

She looks at me as if I've gone mad. "Still, you don't need to go around calling me Cruz's future bride."

It's my turn to consider her sanity. "Cruz is next in line to rule when José hands down his authority and retires. You're Cruz's girlfriend. Best get used to it all."

She balks at me. "Am not! Santos is my boyfriend."

"Right. And Cruz is your..." I wait for Adelita to fill in the blank, but she seals her lips shut like a petulant child.

Of course, Tavita doesn't mind Adelita's sass at all. She even goes one further and starts rubbing Adelita's forearm. It's like she can't stop being sweet to her sister. "What am I missing?" Tavita asks.

"Cruz is my complication." Adelita rubs her forehead with her free hand. "Maybe he's my boyfriend. But don't say it like that."

"Like what?"

"Like he's my boyfriend! It's something he and I should talk about with Santos before everyone up and starts telling me my role in the tribe. I'm not even a legal citizen, much less part of Cáceres' royal family." Her upper lip curls like the very idea is disgusting.

"You call me 'Tio Bruno'," I protest.

"Everyone I know calls you that."

"Yes, everyone who is my nephew or niece calls me that. Well spotted. You're my niece. I'm your uncle. You're in love with two men, and they're both smitten with you. Deal with it. You'll marry Cruz because the tribe will need an heir to make sure the bloodline continues. None of this is new news. None of this is bad news. It's very good news, because it means you'll have a very good life." My neck shrinks. "Except for the whole Máximo part. Nothing I can do about that, other than take the bastard out. I haven't worked up a plan for that just yet."

Tavita shakes her head at me, smirking like she can't believe I don't pull punches. "Well, aren't you a barrel of charm. Always talk to women just like that when you're implying what they should do with their uterus. The harsher the better. Have you told her the name you've picked out for her daughter?"

It'll be a son, but I don't mention that. Women can't hold the ruling spot in the tribe. Tradition demands it.

My face sours. "Maybe I could've said all of that better. But it's no less true."

Tavita catches my eye in the rearview mirror. "Back off, Beautiful. Adelita can fill in the blanks for her own life well enough."

Heat coils through my body, flaring my nostrils

while I grip the steering wheel. I'm not angry Tavita talked back to me. I've never been more turned on in my life. She calls me beautiful, like I'm her pet. I'll be whatever she wants, if only she'll stick around.

Adelita frowns at me, but I ignore her frustration. "Cruz and I are figuring things out. Santos is my boyfriend, and that fact isn't going to change, no matter what Cruz and I decide. Don't make it all weird and start talking about my future before I've even had a chance to consider it. That's too much pressure."

"A conversation is too much pressure? Consuela dressed you up like a bride and gave you a family heirloom to wear around your neck. Eva had a new bed brought in to fit the three of you. And that little nightgown you were wearing? It's not exactly what I would wear if I was trying to keep things platonic."

Adelita giggles, which I'm not expecting. "Just how many pink silk nightgowns do you own, Tio Bruno?"

"Hilarious. You know what I mean."

Tavita switches to massaging Adelita's other arm. "Sounds like you're enjoying your life," Tavita comments wistfully. There's not a hint of jealousy, only a contentment that her sister has been granted moments of happiness, unconventional though they are.

"Other than the whole Máximo thing, I am. Now

there's one less Kalku faction out there, so life is looking sunnier every day."

"So sunny that you want to take another bite of your taco?"

Adelita grimaces, gearing herself up for the battle that comes each time she tries to keep down a morsel of food.

"Don't listen to Bruno," Tavita says sweetly to Adelita, again speaking to her younger sister as if she's a child. "I'm sure you, Cruz and Santos will work things out well enough."

Adelita chews thoughtfully. "How many factions of the Kalku are there? Like, how many more caves of them?"

It's not a totally left field question, but it surprises me all the same. "We don't know. Could be ten more, could be a hundred more. It's hard to track down their locations. At one point, we took to random mountain climbing just to see if we could stumble upon one of their caves."

"And they all answer to Máximo?"

Tavita takes this one. "From how I saw it, they all send reports to him on specific things he asks for. Like, when they tracked you, the Kalku would send reports about your life to Máximo, so he could formulate a plan to have them bring you in. But they do their own things, too. They don't exist solely to do Máximo's bidding, though I've never seen them deny him, either."

I like her summary, though it paints a grim picture. I need to question Tavita so we can learn more about Máximo. But again, pushing her when she's not a day out from having been rescued doesn't hardly seem right. I want to be many things to her, but never cruel.

"Then it's two different plans," Adelita says, thinking aloud. "We need to take down Máximo for sure, but that won't disband everything right away, because the Kalku factions can exist without him. So we need to go for the legs first, cut off Máximo's reach. Then go for the head."

The fact that she's planning out raids has me putting the brakes on this conversation. Though, she's not wrong. "First off, 'we' aren't going to do anything. You two are staying put in Cáceres. The tribe will protect you. If you go running straight to the Kalku, that's exactly what they want. All it takes is for one raid to go south, and you're being shipped over to Máximo's island."

"I can help," Adelita snarls. "I'm not useless."

"However you tricked Cruz into letting you go on missions with the guys isn't going to work on me. You're not a soldier, Adelita, so you'll stay in Cáceres. Put your feet up. Grow Cruz's baby."

Okay, I added that last part just to make her angry.

"You are such an ass!"

Tavita is uncommonly still as she regards Adelita. "You haven't told him."

Adelita squirms in her seat like a child. "It's not his business."

That has my foot reaching for the brake. My back started aching around hour five in the car, so I could use the reprieve anyway. I don't know how Cruz does this all the time, driving for days on end. I should really make sure he takes longer stretches in between missions.

I veer toward the side of the freeway, slowing us to a stop. I put the car in park and turn in my seat, glaring at the both of them.

Though, instantly, I regret directing any anger at Tavita.

"Look, you two. I get that you're not used to tribe life, but secrets can sink us faster than anything. We are happy to keep you safe, but we can't do that if we don't know what's coming for us. So whatever it is, spill it. I don't want any surprises when it comes to your safety."

Tavita reaches forward and strokes my cheek. "I know. I'm sorry I made you worry. I couldn't talk before, or Máximo would overhear. But I won't keep things from you anymore."

Her touch settles the bear that comes to life whenever my authority is questioned. I lean into her caress without meaning to soften so much, and with an audience, no less.

"I need you safe." I hate that I admit the weakness aloud. "I'll tear off the head of every last member of the Kalku if it'll give you a better life."

Tavita's thumb brushes over the seam of my lips, and before I can overthink it, she cranes her body forward. My entire being revs and simultaneously settles when her mouth touches down on mine. It's a feather of a kiss, but it's there and it's ours.

The urge to leap over the console and into the backseat rages in my loins, but I keep still, letting her control the beginning and end.

My forehead presses to hers, and for a moment, I forget the world as we exhale together. I never knew my world could make concessions for such things as breathing.

Tavita kisses my lips once more, and I can taste her trepidation. She's nervous, but unwilling to hang back and let that take over. I love that about her. She feels it all, but moves forward anyway.

I need to shave. I need to shower. I need to suck on a mint. I need to be better than I am for her, yet here she is, kissing me like none of that matters.

When Tavita pulls back to touch her lips, I search her face for signs of flight. But her tongue merely wets her lower lip before a coquettish smile takes over and aims itself right at me.

And just like that, I'm done for. I'm completely and utterly hers.

Adelita's hand covers her mouth, her eyes as wide as saucers. "Holy... what the heck was that?"

Tavita giggles at my glower. "That was awesome, is what it was." Then she sits back with a cocky grin on her face that matches mine. "I'll tell you what, Beautiful. You want to know Adelita's secret? You'll have to arm wrestle her for it. If she wins, she gets to keep her secret. If you win, Adelita talks. Sound fair?"

Adelita glowers at her sister. "You know that's nothing like a good idea. He'll get what he wants either way."

I slap my hands together. "I love it. Let's do that. You and me, Adelita. Let's use the hood of the car for balance."

I open up my door before she can protest any further. I check for traffic before stepping out and helping Adelita from the car. She's still too slight, her color too pallid. This is hardly going to be fair, but as Adelita doesn't seem to be putting up too much more of a fight to counter the suggestion, I go with my advantage. She was well enough (barely) to be discharged from the hospital, but the doctor only agreed to it when I promised to follow strict bedrest for her.

After arm wrestling.

I can't help my smirk as I rest my elbow on the hood of the car, extending my hand to grasp her dainty palm.

"This is a bad idea," she murmurs, shooting daggers at her sister.

Tavita shrugs, as if she couldn't care less.

"I'll be gentle," I promise. "I won't hurt you."

Adelita purses her lips as she casts me a look laced with sass and sheer frustration. "I'm sure you won't."

Tavita stands beside her sister, her hand on her back to brace her in case she's unsteady on her feet. I suddenly feel like a tool for asking my niece to stand at all, much less arm wrestle. She just got out of the emergency room a handful of hours ago. Sure, she can keep down food now and she hasn't fainted in a while, but still, I'm not a complete ass.

Or maybe I am, since I'm going through with this.

I count us off and expect a quick victory, followed by some answers. Instead what I get is an immoveable wall.

"What... I don't... What are you doing?" I grit my teeth and use my abdomen to bolster my muscle, but still, her puny arm doesn't budge.

She's evoking deep breathing, but something tells me it's only to keep herself upright. "This is embarrassing," she murmurs, then she amends with a quick, "for both of us, not just you. If I wasn't so weak, this wouldn't be taking so long."

I'm sweating, confused and on the edge of demanding answers now. When the back of my hand inches toward the hood of the car, my curiosity wins out over my need to dominate, so I give up the fight.

She slams my hand to the car, dissatisfied even though I'm completely floored.

I don't beat around the bush. "How did you do that? You beat me at arm wrestling? I don't…"

Adelita still looks like the breeze might blow her over. "Yesterday, I couldn't have. Dehydration is the pits."

Tavita's maternal tone comes out with a flourish. "Let's get you back in the car, honey girl. You don't need to be on your feet for this long." She fusses over Adelita, but I'm the one with the keys.

I slide into the front seat, shaking out my wrist. "Talk, woman."

"Drive, man," Adelita spouts back.

"Not until I get my answers. In fact, I'm more than happy to sit here all day long."

Adelita hangs her head, and Tavita massages the nape of her neck. The two cuddle into each other like twin animals seeking warmth.

When Adelita finally speaks, her voice is quiet. "I've got crazy strength."

She says it like she's confessing to a crime.

"Come again? Don't make me ask for more information. You know that's going to make me frustrated. Tell me the whole story."

Adelita shivers into Tavita's side. "I was born this way. Mom and I kept it quiet because we didn't know what it meant. Or maybe she did. Máximo is the one who got her pregnant. I don't know how much she knew about him, but if she knew even five percent of this whole crazy other world you've got going on here, then she probably had her suspicions he wasn't totally human. Either way, I'm pretty strong."

Tavita tuts her.

Adelita huffs. "Fine. I can tear a car door off its hinges. That kind of strong. When my mother died in the bus crash, Santiago was supposed to take me to Máximo, but he didn't. Instead he capped my strength. Said I would only be as strong as I was gentle. Guess that was his way of putting a limit to how horribly Máximo could use me. Though, I've murdered on the road with the guys a couple times and my strength is still here, so maybe Santiago's blessing was a bust."

"You killed someone on the road? Who?"

She shrugs. "I don't know their names. The Kalku

members who attacked us. I fought back. I didn't want to, but it was either him or me, so I made the choice for us both."

"I'm not sure self-defense cancels out a gentle spirit," Tavita says.

Dozens of facts and events flicker through my mind as I start up the car and get back on the road. "Good that you told me, Adelita. You should have told me the second you entered Cáceres. I need to know who's in my tribe."

Adelita snaps her mouth shut, though I can tell she has opinions on that.

"So that's why the guys had such a hard time bringing you home when you ran away. They can't just drag you back."

She scoffs. "Santos would never do something so cruel."

I bite back my retort, wanting to spout back that Santos was raised in cruelty, and is certainly no stranger to it. Perhaps such restraint means that I'm maturing. Better late than never, I guess.

I thumb the steering wheel. "So that's the reason La Sayona is afraid of you and leaves Cruz alone if you're near. Cruz sleeping soundly is such a blessing that no one wants to look too closely at the reason why, but that makes sense."

Adelita bristles. "La Sayona should know better than to torment the mind of a sweet man who's done nothing to deserve her vengeance."

I snigger at her description of my surly nephew. People often say he's more my son than José's, judging by his un-sunny disposition. "I like that you think Cruz is sweet. You're wrong, but I like it. He needs someone to remind him to live a little."

"You're one to talk."

A hardness sweeps over my features. "Yeah, in fact, I am the authority on that subject. I don't want him to end up like me any more than you do. So keep thinking Cruz is sweet. Maybe one day, he will be."

Adelita shifts in her seat. Her dislike of me is in no danger of dissipating, which I find amusing.

Then something else clicks into place. I slam the flat of my hand to the steering wheel. "You're the one who pulled out the curse axe, not Cruz! Santos is free from his curse of being mute because of you!"

Her head darts around, as if she's afraid someone might overhear. "That's not public information, okay? Cruz pulled it out, as far as anyone else is concerned."

"Why don't you want the credit?"

"You say 'credit,' I say 'target on my back.'"

Tavita nods. "It's true. You're part of Father's plan,

Adelita. That's what Máximo wants you for. Or, well, part of it, anyway."

Adelita and I both pin Tavita with our surprise. "What?"

Tavita keeps an arm around Adelita, but her face loses its sunshine. Her mind isn't with us; it's back on the island. "Máximo wants you to undo his curse."

I pull the old story from my memory. "'Whatever Máximo most desires will be just out of his reach.'"

"That's the one. If Father ever gets you onto his island, that's what he's going to have you do." Her arm tightens around Adelita. "Whatever you do, you cannot give him what he wants. It would be better for us all to die than to give the world over to the lust of a madman like him."

12

EVA'S WISH
ADELITA

I have never been fussed over so much in my life. Mama was good at taking care of me when I fell ill, but living with Don José and Consuela is like living with Mama multiplied. Before I can ask for a drink of water, it's already being brought to me.

Chef Aarón feels responsible (though I've already told him it wasn't his fault the steamed milks he brought us were poisoned), so he's been by my bedside since I came home.

Home.

Never thought I'd say that about Cáceres.

I'm in my own bedroom, not Cruz's, and every time I shift in the bed or reach for something, Chef Aarón is on his feet to help me.

Aarón. He asked me to call him Aarón, not Chef Aarón.

I'm guessing he's in his sixties, what with the crinkles around his eyes and the lines on his forehead, but there's a dexterity and liveliness to him that suggests he doesn't sit down much.

Eva knocks on my door and then lets herself in. "Hey, sis. I brought you a cold compress. Mom said you were looking flushed. She's doing breakfast with the littles in the kitchen."

Though I can't imagine I'm feverish, I let Eva fuss over me. She straightens my covers on all four corners, and then does the motion again, flitting around my bedside with a worried set to her lips.

She needs to talk. This concern isn't all for my "fragile state," as they keep calling it. Something happened.

"Aarón, would you mind giving me a few minutes with Eva?"

"Of course." But he hesitates once he stands. "But you will call for me if you need anything, yes?"

"You're first on the list."

He leans over and presses his lips to my forehead. "I'm so sorry, *hija*. I wasn't careful enough."

I catch his hand, really hoping he hears me this

time. "It's not your fault. Let's be angry at Máximo together. I think we're stronger that way."

The corner of his mouth lifts, though I can tell he's nowhere near being ready to let himself off the hook for my poisoning. "I'll go start on your dinner. What would you like?"

"You brought me the hugest lunch in history, so something small would be nice. Whatever you've got left over in the fridge. I'm not picky."

He narrows one eye at me, and then touches my nose. "Leftovers? What do you take me for? Do you know why I work here?"

I spread out my arms and shrug my palms skyward. "The circus wasn't hiring?" He scoffs at my slight tease.

Aarón jerks his thumb to his chest. "Because I am the best chef in Cáceres. Do not suggest leftovers. Not when you've got a master at your service. What do you want, *hija*? Anything at all."

A smile cracks my face. I can't help it. "I'm a big fan of breakfast for dinner. Do you have breakfast things?"

He crosses his arms and leans back, as if I've challenged him. "Can I make breakfast? In my sleep. How does eggs and chorizo sound? Pancakes with cinnamon and sugar?"

"You're punishing yourself by spoiling me," I point out. "This wasn't your fault, Aarón." No matter how many times I tell him, I'm certain he won't hear me until he's ready. Still, I want my words to play in his head on a loop, so I'll repeat them until he clings to their message of redemption.

"Eggs and pancakes. Coming right up." Then he turns to Eva. "Have you had your afternoon coffee yet, *hija*?"

"I'm too wired for coffee, but thanks. I fixed you your cup and left it next to the griddle just before I came in here. Extra sweetened condensed milk, just how you like it when you're stressed."

He lays the flat of his hand to his chest. "You're too good to me, Eva."

"I happen to think I'm just the right amount of perfect." When Eva sits on the bed by my side and leans against the headboard, she smiles up at him, looking like a little girl. "I wouldn't say no to some of those eggs, though."

Aarón gives her a short bow. "Anything you like, my dear."

I love how sweet everyone is to each other. No one is an inconvenience. No one is an imposition. Everyone takes care of each other.

...except for me, who isn't allowed out of bed. I'd almost finagled a walk around the house, but then Tavita came in with her physical therapy degree and experience and trumped all that. Apparently, the doctor's orders aren't something we're allowed to blow off in this house. Usually, if Mom or I broke down and absolutely *had* to go to the doctor, we'd do the bare minimum of obedience and go back to work as soon as the ink dried on the doctor's note.

Perhaps that wasn't the best way.

After all the running from the Kalku, being chucked in the pit, and being scared for my life, spending the day in bed is just the ticket.

Eva cuddles in beside me, her perfume sweet but not too heady. I flip the comforter's edge down, and she tucks her legs under the covering. "You feeling alright?" she asks, her back against the headboard next to me, her shoulder bumping mine.

"I'm doing well. I'm more worried about all the things on your mind. What's up?"

She sighs, as if she's been waiting for me to ask so she could unburden herself. "An offer from one of the soldiers came in while you were gone." When I quirk my brow for more information, she says, "He asked for my hand in marriage."

I settle into therapist-mode, which fits me like a glove and makes me feel more like myself. "How do you feel about that?"

She shrugs. I can tell she's been waiting for me to be

here so we could piece out the mess together, examining one puzzle fragment at a time. "I've spoken with the man exactly four times in my life. If I married him, it wouldn't be like what Dad and Mom have. It wouldn't be what you have with…" She doesn't finish the sentence, placing me with either guy, which I guess is wise. Eva leans her head on my shoulder. "I'm a bargaining chip. That's why he proposed. He wants to sit on the council with Dad and Cruz. I'm not his wife; I'm his stepping stone."

Gross. Though I want to state my reaction aloud, I've learned that's not my place. "What do you know about the guy who asked for your hand?"

"No more than I did the others. He sent over his standing in the military, along with any past misdeeds, and a statement of his wealth."

"So, a bank statement and any notes to the principal?" I should really hide my true feelings better, but this whole conversation has me reeling.

My small sentence sends me on a coughing fit. My throat is still intermittently dry, so Eva rushes to my cup of water and presses it to my lips. "You need to have small sips every couple of minutes," Eva chides, repeating the advice the healer, the doctor and Tavita broadcasted to the house.

I should be grateful for the overzealous care, and I

probably am. But being fawned over by an entire family is new to me.

Once Eva is satisfied I've had enough water, she resumes her spot beside me in the bed, leaning her back against the headboard. "I can't believe I'm actually considering it."

"Really?"

"It would make Dad happy. Dad does the legwork with these things. Sometimes Tio Bruno will investigate my prospects a little. Both of them gave their approval, which is rare. Usually one of them finds a flaw they warn me about, so I can beg off. So either there is no glaring flaw with this guy, or..."

She lets me fill in the blank. "Or they just want to see you married, regardless of who it's to."

"Bingo."

My words settle in the air between us, and for once, I begin to understand her conundrum, and why any woman would agree to such a thing.

Eva loves her family. She cares for them enough to give her future over to a stranger. I wonder if I would have done that to please my mom, were she still alive.

A niggling thought chases in on the heels of that one: my mom loved me too much to ever entertain sending me off to a man I didn't know. Though admittedly, we'd never been in that scenario, still my soul is certain that I was her treasure. She would go down to the grave protecting me above all else.

Sadness settles in that Eva does not have this same certainty with her family.

"How can I help?" It's the only useful thing I can think to say. Telling a client what to do isn't in my job description. Self-actualization is only possible if one learns to make healthy decisions for the future without being told the "correct" answer.

Plus, "correct" is often relative.

Eva cuddles into my side. "Listening to me blather is helpful." Her head leans on my shoulder as she sighs with plenty of flourish. "If only you could tell me not to do it, and then go with me to Dad to tell him I want to get married for love, even it takes the next fifty years."

I chuckle at how well I've been played. "You could have just asked, you know."

She giggles, her arm banding around my stomach. "Well, it's a lot to ask."

"No, it's not." I touch my toe to hers. "I wish you could meet a man who had no political prowess to gain by being with you. Then you would know for sure it's love. Is there something like that? What about a prince from the Mendez tribe or the other tribe?"

A flash of insecurity flits over her features. "Dad would never approve of an outsider. If I could marry the prince from the Anzaldúa tribe..." A secretive smile teases her lips. "But that's not an option."

There's someone else. Someone from outside of Cáceres. I don't call Eva on the crime, but I see it clearly. She's smitten with someone her family won't approve of. Whomever this prince from Anzaldúa is, perhaps.

I bump my shoulder to hers. "Hello, I'm an outsider, and my new nickname is Cruz's Future Bride."

Eva fiddles with the edge of the comforter. "Yes, but before you, we all thought Cruz was destined to die alone. For Cruz, it will be you or no one, because of La Sayona." She catches her words after they've already hit the air. "And obviously because Cruz is head over heels for you. I, on the other hand, will be marrying a soldier Tio Bruno picks out. Fun times."

I ignore the insinuation lingering in her teasing tone. Cruz and I are getting used to each other. No use making it more than what it is. Just because my stomach lions claw to get near him doesn't mean a thing.

"Trust your gut, Eva. If you don't want to marry him, you owe it to the both of you not to go through with it."

"I wish Dad could do that listening thing you do."

I chuckle at my unremarkable superpower. "That listening thing I do? Anybody can listen."

"Not the way you do."

When a heavy knock announces we have a visitor,

Eva brushes off her nerves with a cool confidence she keeps on tap at all times. "Come in," she beckons.

Don José comes in, but his usual breezy smile is nowhere to be found.

I sit up straighter, my shoulders at the top of the headboard. "Are you alright?"

The corner of his mouth lifts. "You are a good person to ask me that. Rafi called. There have been some developments with my boys."

I love that he calls them his boys.

I finger the coverlet, my mouth drawing to the side while I wait for him to reveal the reason he's lost the pep in his step. "How are they?"

His long sigh does nothing to assuage my growing concern. "Santos and Cruz finally stopped vomiting, and the doctors have them on their way to rehydration, so that's promising. But while Cruz was in the hospital, he had a particularly bad bout with La Sayona."

Eva whimpers while I go into full alert. "I knew I should have gone to the hospital. Can I borrow one of the cars? I can go to him. When I'm around, La Sayona doesn't go near him."

Though Cruz told me his family knows about our odd connection, we don't often speak of my role so openly.

Don José closes his eyes and rests his hand atop

mine. "It gives me great peace to hear you are so ready to help my son. You are the thing my heart needs, *hija.* Thank you. There's no need for you to take a car, though. Rafi has the boys and they are on their way here. But what happened in the hospital was most troubling." His eyes go out of focus, and I can tell he's slipping into a memory. "When La Sayona haunted me, it was torture from the time I slipped into unconsciousness until the moment I woke. It wasn't often, but on occasion, she would mark me, and I would wake with a remnant token of her punishments." He glances at his fingers. "She cut off all my fingers one night, and in the morning, I had bruises across my knuckles."

Eva is a ball of nerves beside me, her fingers digging into her forearm as she holds herself through her father's story.

"Before you came along, Cruz had a few times like that, where he would wake with her marks on his body. Cruz doesn't like to talk about any of it, so honestly, it could be loads of times, and I only know about the ones I see. But usually La Sayona torments his mind and leaves his body alone." Don José clears his throat, and for the first time, I notice the bags under his eyes. "While Cruz was in the hospital, he experienced sleep paralysis. Where he was awake, but he couldn't move for several minutes when he first woke up."

My mind flips through all the facts I know about sleep paralysis. "That must've been so scary for him."

"More than scary," José whispers, his voice cracking. "Cruz stopped breathing. For a minute and a half, he couldn't breathe and couldn't move. It's lucky Rafi was watching both of them so closely, or he might not have seen it. The doctor was able to get him out of it, but it was an ordeal and he had to be intubated."

Eva's lower lip quivers. "What does this mean, Dad?"

José answers Eva, but it's my eyes his gaze locks in on. "It means that La Sayona is getting stronger."

HOMECOMING
ADELITA

The ice in my veins shoots me into action. "If La Sayona is strong enough to give Cruz sleep paralysis and get him to stop breathing, then I need to go to him now. I need to meet them on the road, just in case he dozes off on the way."

I flip the coverlet off my legs, but Don José holds up his hand to stave off my hurry. "Just hearing you say that puts a significant piece of my worry at ease. That you would be willing to help my son?" He palms his sternum. "Anything you want, it's yours."

I lean forward. "I want to get to the guys. You said they're on their way home, yes?"

"They are, so there's no use going out to meet them. They'll be here soon enough. Rafi signed them out against the doctor's advice because dehydration is a danger, yes, but Cruz cannot be exposed to La Sayona again. He is coming here to get some sleep."

The heavy implication falls between us, tearing away the veil of "we just so happen to like having you around" to reveal the desperation of a family who loves Cruz.

Don José's voice is hoarse as he holds my gaze with unconcealed anxiety. "Will you help my son?"

This family kills me with how much they love each other. It's incredible to watch the beam of need radiating off this great man, and now his daughter.

I cover Don José's hand with my own. "Of course. I'll do whatever I can to keep La Sayona away from Cruz."

Don José's eyes close. "It's unfair of me to ask this of you, but I am a desperate man. I would do anything for my son, but this is the one thing I cannot do for him. Whatever you want, it is yours. Ask for your heart's desire, and I will make it so. For saving my son from my father's demon?" He taps his sternum. "Anything. Everything."

I should think it through. I should pass on the offer.

Instead, I blurt out an answer not even I am expecting. "Citizenship. I want citizenship in Cáceres."

I expect hesitation. I expect a fight. Instead, Don José

nods once. "I've already started the paperwork. You'll need to sign it when it's completed, but of course."

I blink at him, wondering now just how immovable those walls are. They're letting me in and giving me citizenship without being married to anyone here or adopted into a family.

This is good. This is progress. Hopefully I will be the first of many who add new color and flavor to Cáceres.

Eva reaches toward me and tips the cup to my lips, making sure I drink every few minutes, even when I forget. "Rafi said he checked the guys out against the doctor's orders? What state are they in?"

"Cruz and Santos are dehydrated, so I've called a healer in to give them a look the second they get back. They should be here sometime in the night. Probably around two or three in the morning."

My nose wrinkles. "Cruz will stay awake that long?"

Eva sets the cup back down. "He'll have to."

Don José motions around the room. "This is your bedroom. Would you like me to send Cruz in here when he gets home?"

I gnaw on my lower lip, unsure how to say what I need to. "This might be hard for you to hear, but Santos, Cruz and I sometimes... On the road we've been..."

Everyone knows the odd arrangement, but I haven't put words to it to Cruz's father yet.

Don José holds up his hand. "Would you prefer to sleep in Cruz's bedroom tonight? The larger bed might suit the three of you better."

I gust out my relief. "Thank you for not making me say it."

Don José smirks at me. "I'll get Cruz's room ready and set up the healer in there. She'll check in on you again, too."

My legs swing off the bed, but Eva stops me. "Not so fast, Sis. You're still on bedrest. That means you and I sit here and get waited on like the princesses we are, and everyone else does the heavy lifting."

I narrow an eye at her. "That is not going to happen. I can be useful."

José stands and tucks me back in with steady hands.

I wonder if this is what it's like to have a dad.

"Eva is right. You were taken into the Kalku's cave. You were thrown into a pit. You were poisoned and starved. And yet you still have the grace to come to our family's aide by helping Cruz." He leans in and kisses my forehead. "There is nothing more to do."

I highly doubt that, but I don't argue any further.

The next few hours give me a peek into the life of a princess. After the best breakfast-for-dinner I've ever had, the housekeeper draws me a bath, which no one has done for me since I was a little girl. The water is scented with oils that smell like lavender and something that reminds me of baby powder.

When I get out, Consuela helps me get dressed in one of the silk nightgowns that fits me like a sexy slip. Luckily, she slides a peach silk bathrobe over my shoulders. The hem tickles the tops of my knees when I walk toward the vanity. Consuela sits me down and proceeds to brush out my tangles.

Consuela hums while she fusses over me, like my snarls are no trouble at all. Like she doesn't have three little kids, an adult daughter and three sons who have just been through the wringer. I know those things are on her heart, but she still has the peace of mind to pour out kindness onto me.

Consuela runs the brush through my hair over and over without the slightest hint of impatience, just like my mom used to do. Though I've just indulged in the most relaxing bath ever, sadness creeps into my psyche as I watch Consuela in the mirror.

"What are you thinking about?" she asks me without meeting my gaze in the reflective glass.

I debate saying the predictable "nothing," but she deserves better than that from me. "I miss my mother," I admit. "No one's brushed my hair and drawn me a bath in a very long time."

Consuela's strokes slow. "What was she like?"

How can you possibly sum up a person like Mom? "She could make a game out of anything. Conjure up happiness out of nothing. She was perfect."

Consuela finishes with my hair and then checks my nails for signs of wear. "Sounds like it. Do you think she would like the bathrobe? Good enough for her best girl?"

I glance down. "She would think I was the fanciest woman in the world with this on. She'd make a huge fuss."

Consuela smiles. "Did she have a favorite color? Maybe I can get you a robe in that shade, so you can feel close to her when you wear it."

Her thoughtfulness tugs at my insides. "Me," I admit, my neck shrinking. "I'm her favorite color." I point to my eyes.

Consuela picks up my water cup and molds my fingers around it. "She sounds like a good mother."

"How about you?"

"I hope I am a good mother. Some days I think I'm getting the hang of it. Other days, I'm certain I'm failing. I suppose that's how it goes, though."

"No, I meant to ask about your mother. If she had a favorite color and whatnot."

There's a tightness to Consuela as her gaze tears away, suddenly fixated on the box of ribbons on the vanity. "I know I was never my mother's favorite color. I don't like to think about my life before I met José. He is good to me in a way I never dreamed goodness could exist."

I reach out and hold onto her hand, hoping she doesn't flit from me in an effort to run from the pain. "I'm glad you're here."

Consuela meets my eyes again. "Funny. I was just going to say the same about you."

I have loads more questions, but I don't think now is the time for them. Plus, it's all idle curiosity. Consuela's past is none of my business.

When I yawn, she helps me to Cruz's bedroom. My limbs are still tight from dehydration. No matter how often I drink water, everything still hurts, and I have limited mobility. She's patient with me, though, and doesn't hurry me along.

Consuela stays with me while the healer checks me from head to toe, as she's done several times since I got back. "Your progress is slow," she scolds, as if it's my fault. "You are not drinking enough."

Bedrest isn't even close to being lifted for me, she informs me. I try not to whine aloud.

When the healer and Consuela leave me for the

night, I drift off the same way I did the evening before—in a series of fits and turns that accompany anxiety. I'm not a fan of the dark now, but I'm too embarrassed to ask for a nightlight or something.

At midnight, I reach with a trembling hand and flick on the lamp, resigning myself to the fact that I might not be able to sleep peacefully in the dark for a while. I don't want to think about the pit. I don't want to dwell on how scared I was for Tavita, that she might never wake up. I'm frightened of the sharpened teeth of the warriors, and the impassive look on the cave father's face as he ordered us to be lowered into the pit. I think of all the other women who were down there before me, whose journeys ended with their hearts being torn from their chests so the organ could be boiled.

I'm a fantastic listener, but I never learned how to talk about my problems.

And so they build, compounding in my head and heart until they develop into full-fledged psychosis.

Panic quickens my breaths until the tears build up pressure behind my eyes. When they fall, I finally grant myself the space to give a small voice to the fear that threatens to take me over. In the back of my mind, I am grateful I'm hydrated enough finally to cry. I'm getting better, or at least my body is on its way to healing.

My heart might take a bit longer to repair.

I'm no good at sleeping alone anymore. Though I've slept by myself for most of my life, these past several weeks have spoiled me for life. I toss and turn under the glow of the lamp, wishing for Santos' strong and lithe body to ground me so I don't drift away completely.

My dreams are scattered, and feature a giant upward reaching tunnel that gives way to a faceless foe. He looks down on me, disapproving and smug.

Even in my dreams, I am not good enough for my father. I shouldn't want to impress him, and even in this subconscious platform, I scold myself for the folly.

The scenery is whooshed away when the bedroom door opens. The form I would know even in shadow fills my vision. "Santos," I breathe, grateful for so many things, but most of all, for him.

He saved me from my nightmare, which is no great surprise. He saves me from the bad things constantly.

Santos is thinner, and there are bags under his eyes. Even in the dim light, I can pick out how haunted he looks. As he nears the bed, I don't sit up; I simply hold my arms out, inviting him to rest with me.

He takes the offer without pause, climbing into the enormous raised bed so he can scoop me into his arms. He's clumsy with my body, which is so unlike him that I worry he shouldn't have left the doctor's care. "Santos, you need a healer. Honey, talk to me."

But he can't. At least, not yet. He lays on his back while I prop myself up on my elbow to stare down at him. I brush a few strands of hair from his forehead, noting the sheer overwhelm on his features.

It's too much. He's been through enough. His twin is alive, which should be cause for celebration, but Santiago is being held captive on the island with Máximo. I know Santos enough to understand that he will not be okay until he finds a way to liberate his brother.

Which might not be entirely possible.

My lips touch down on his forehead, respecting his pain as it ricochets through his body. I can see echoes of terror in his eyes, so I rub the space between his eyebrows, reminding his face, at least, that he is in a safe place, and we will figure this out together.

Somehow.

I hope.

Something about my touch brings him back to the present, instead of lost in the abyss as he's been. His hand is weak, but it reaches up and cups my wrist. He uses the paltry leverage to lower my torso atop his.

Santos kisses like an angel who has known true torment. Every exquisite brush of his lips brings about a flurry of beauty that flies around me like a swirl of autumn leaves. I'm lost in the flavor of him, blind to the world because he tastes like peppermint and pure kindness—the combination I've been searching for my whole life.

Kissing Santos is like coming home to myself. He loves me in a way I never thought I should demand of the world, giving graciously and freely without wondering what's in it for him.

I am what's in it for him, and for some reason, he thinks that's enough.

My thumb brushes across his cheekbone as my tongue slides across his. He's delicious, and I've been starved for the taste of him. He lets me control the pace of our reunion, giving whatever my lips, tongue and touch demand. He makes it clear with his submissive body language that he is mine for the taking. He trusts me to be careful with him, so I do my best to consider the long road he has traveled without a guide.

My fingers trill slowly down his throat, which awakens the rest of his body. Santos twists under the sheets when I touch on his chest, letting loose sweet moaning sounds that tell me he's needed the closeness just as much as I have.

When my hand reaches his stomach, Santos pauses our kiss to take off his shirt, which is the best reason to pull away from a kiss. Our lips meet again, only this time, it's with intent for something more than sweetness. He places my hand back on his torso, where we left off, letting me know he very much wants my fingers roaming his body.

Don't mind if I do.

14

WHAT I NEED

ADELITA

Stroking Santos' stomach gives me great pleasure. The hard planes of his abdomen are the things naughty dreams are made of. Saving me from my nightmare is the quest for which his body is well equipped. His muscles jump to meet my fingertips, his breath syncopating as our kiss picks up its pace to match my thumping heartbeat. We haven't spoken of all the tragedies that have torn us apart these past few days. I haven't heard the report from his doctor, or listened to him unburden himself.

Yet still we find a way to connect.

My fingers drag along the hemisphere of his trim waistline, teasing and tickling while he deepens the kiss to give me whatever green light I require to keep going.

He tugs on the belt of my robe, opening the pink silk to reveal the lace cupping my breasts.

A soft moan of helpless pleasure escapes his lips, telling me he very much wants all of this and more.

When I pop open the button on his jeans, he doesn't hesitate to slide the pink silk off my shoulders, his lips going for my throat. His mouth suctions harder than I anticipate. My toes curl as pleasure shoots through my body to the tune of Santos' scandalous moans.

I inch his zipper down, giving myself permission to play because our lives have been devoid of pleasure for too many days. The earthy scent of his skin floods my senses, pushing out any hint of the fear that wouldn't leave me alone mere minutes ago.

When the door opens, Santos quickly flips the comforter over my shoulders, shielding me from view of whomever enters without knocking.

Cruz. Of course Cruz wouldn't knock. This is his bedroom.

Or maybe it's ours. I have no idea anymore.

The healer is at Cruz's side. Even as I situate my nightgown under the blanket to more properly cover me, I notice that Cruz is just as haggard as Santos. His steps are dragging and his shoulders are drooped.

"Lady Adelita," the healer greets me. "Santos." She

bobs her head toward Santos. "Master Cruz is well enough to sleep, but not fit for much else. He needs to rest, and he needs hydration. I've checked on his wounds, and I'll be in every few hours to make sure the three of you get some water." She deposits Cruz on my other side in the bed, and moves around the massive mattress to Santos' side. "Your turn, Santos. Let's get you into the other room so I can give your injuries a look."

"Injuries?" I assumed the worst was the poisoning and subsequent dehydration. "Did something happen?"

Santos keeps his eyes from me, so I know it was bad, whatever it was.

The healer gives me a polite smile. "That's all a conversation for daylight. Master Cruz requires rest. He's overdone it on caffeine, and has gone two days without sleep. He needs rest now. Everything else can wait."

Cruz won't look at me. Shame is radiating off him in waves, like he's embarrassed for some reason.

Of course he is. The unsaid sentiment in the room is that he cannot sleep without me now. Cruz doesn't like needing anything, and it's clear to everyone in this house that he has a clear weakness he cannot muscle through alone.

Now Cruz is just like everyone else, needing to lean on others when life gets too hard.

I wish he understood how much of a superhero he still is, even though La Sayona is trying to tear him apart from the inside.

"No," Santos replies, not rudely. "I won't be parted from her. Whatever you need to do, see to it in here."

The healer purses her lips, but nods. "Not a problem. I'll need the full light, though." She flicks on the overhead chandelier (because of course this grand room comes with a chandelier).

I gasp as the overhead light picks up far more than the lamp did. Santos stands, zipping and buttoning his jeans without a hint of smugness or apology to the rest of the room. With his back bared to me, I see several long gouges and the beginnings of bruises littering his muscular frame. "What happened?"

Santos turns his head over his shoulder as the healer checks Santos' vitals, starting with the basics. "We were jumped by the Kalku on the way back. They were waiting outside the hospital. Good timing, actually. Cruz and I were barely upright. You'd think that would make us easy targets, but Rafi was extra motivated. He unleashed on them."

The gravity in his tone is not lost on me. "Fire?" It's my code for asking if Rafi was able to turn into his dragon.

"Not much of a fight if a shifter is properly motivated." Santos shucks his jeans at the healer's request, revealing a few more marks on his shins that dent my tender heart. "Rafi loves us."

It's a firm declaration that rings true throughout the room. Rafi does love them, and would tap into whatever magic might be at his disposal to protect his brothers.

"Is Rafael alright? Where is he?"

Cruz's voice is rough. He's still sitting on the other side of the bed, but hasn't laid down. "They didn't land more than a few blows on him before he cleaned house. He's been driving for way too long, though. We're all beat, baby."

His term of endearment pings a precious part inside of me I try not to show. But I cannot help the blush in my cheeks when Cruz is sweet to me.

The healer answers enough of my worry to put me mildly at ease. "Rafael will be alright. He's suffering from exhaustion, of course, as all three of them are. He sustained a troubling blow to his forearm, but nothing is broken. He's got scrapes and bruises, but he will be alright."

The healer turns Santos around so he's facing me, and starts in on disinfecting the cuts on his back. Santos doesn't even flinch, but I grimace enough for the both of us. I hate when he is in pain, even if he's been conditioned not to show it. In some cases, that's even more troubling—to not express hurt because you've been subjected to so much of the stuff throughout life.

I want to kiss his wounds. My kisses heal people, as we learned when I kissed his cheek and the scarring on his cheek mended.

But another thought chases in on the heels of the first: healing Santos that way is quite painful for him, and takes a long time. He needs sleep more than a closed scrape.

Santos locks his eyes on mine, combing my face for the details he's missed while the healer works on his back and legs. His gaze doesn't move, even as the minutes stack on top of each other. I still under the weight of his inspection. Though my robe is back in place, I let him see me as I am—tired, undernourished and frightened, but here.

"You were stolen," Santos says quietly. "Stolen from my arms."

I swallow hard at the memory I don't want to conjure back up. "Máximo was controlling Tavita. It wasn't her fault. She couldn't stop herself."

He nods once. "Dad mentioned that on the phone." It doesn't seem to alleviate his upset. His stern disapproval doesn't appear to be directed at Tavita, but at himself. Like he somehow failed because he was poisoned and out of commission.

I cannot fathom the stress this man puts on himself.

Minutes tick by as Cruz drinks his glass of water and the healer finishes up with Santos. Finally, the healer packs up her bag while waiting for Santos to drain a glass of water. "Very good. I'll be back in a few hours to wake you and get more fluids in you three."

Santos escorts the healer out and the locks the door. It's an ominous sound, the click, and all it stands for. It means that we cannot trust that the house will not be breached. It's an unease that prickled the hairs on the back of my neck when I came to realize it days ago, but it hits the guys harder. This is their safe haven. This is their home.

"I might need to go for a walk or something," Cruz says, his voice gravelly. "I think I overdid it with the caffeine. I'm exhausted but jittery. It feels like my insides are coming out of my skin."

I climb out of the bed without a stitch of grace, and move to stand in front of him. "You're wobbly on your feet, Cruz. I saw you walk in. Let's get you ready for bed, and then you can make that call. I'll help you."

He frowns uncertainly, as if he doesn't like the idea of the word "help" one bit. "Did Dad tell you about..."

I nod solemnly, moving slow as I tug his shirt over his head. "You're safe now. I'm right here."

Division storms his features. I know he doesn't want to need help like this, but there's also the relief that tonight won't be flooded with torment. That he won't wake to paralysis, suffocation and an impending heart attack.

Compassion swirls in my heart, and before I know it, I'm rubbing his forearms. Cruz truly is jittery to the touch, but the more I massage the meat of his muscles, his shoulders begin to relax.

"She's never going to leave me alone," Cruz whispers. "La Sayona." I can hear true pain radiating out from him into the room.

"No," I counter, holding tight to his hand. "*I'm* never going to leave you alone. We will find a way to chase her out of your mind for good, Cruz."

His lower lip quivers before he inhales and sucks it in, capturing the plump swell between his teeth. He looks so small like this, like a little boy who might always be lost. Cruz nods, closing his eyes as he tugs me to stand between his open knees. "I'm sorry I need you like this."

I motion around his home. "I'm sorry I need you for all of this."

Santos turns off the overhead light and gets into the

bed in only his boxer briefs. He pats the mattress. "Sleep," he commands. "We can punish ourselves in the morning."

I bring Cruz's fist to my mouth, kissing his knuckles before climbing under the covers between them.

Santos rolls me onto my side, spooning my form, as he likes to do. But I can tell his anxiety isn't forgotten. His leg curves over both of mine, trapping my thighs between his. Santos snakes his arm around my torso like a seatbelt, the back of his hand pressed against my cheek atop my pillow to cradle my head.

"Santos, my heart, I can't sleep like this."

Santos loosens his grip, but only enough for me to draw a full breath. "Any looser, and you'll be snatched away. I can't risk it."

I shouldn't chuckle. Nothing about his scenario is funny. But I can't help myself. Santos is sweet in a way most people don't let themselves become after life throws them such turmoil. "I thought you said we could wait to punish ourselves in the morning. It's not your fault, you know. If Máximo wants to get at me, there's precious little any of us can do to stop him."

"I'm here, Santos," Cruz says quietly as he stands to take his jeans off. Then he grimaces. "Of course, that did little good the last time. She was taken when I was right next to her. To both of you."

I purse my lips, not loving this unhealthy road we're traveling down. Once Cruz has stripped down to his underwear, I reach for his arm, tugging him to lay beside me. "We can't help that. Tonight is for sleeping. Tomorrow is for worrying about things we cannot control."

Cruz's eyes flicker with raw emotion that the glow from the lamp picks up with contrasting shadows and light. "I lost you."

"Never," I promise. "We'll always have each other."

And I truly mean it. The four of us are enmeshed, not just in this mess, but in the happiness we've managed to find along the way.

To seal my vow, I tell them the one thing I know they're not expecting. "Your dad is working on my citizenship papers. Cáceres is going to be my home now. I'm not going anywhere."

A mix of surprise and wonder flits over Cruz's features.

It's the wrong moment for our first kiss, but it finds us all the same. It's nothing as intense as the makeout session Santos and I entertained, but when Cruz's lips touch on mine, the part of me I thought might always remain unsettled clicks into place.

His lips are gentle with me, which wouldn't have been my first guess. Cruz seems like the "pillage first, ask for directions later" kind of guy. But this kiss isn't confident and smoldering; it's precious and perfect.

And it's over far too quickly.

Cruz reaches over my body and grips the nape of Santos' neck, meeting his gaze with apology. "I tried to stay away."

Santos responds by removing his arm from around me so he can cup Cruz's bicep. "I don't know why. This makes sense."

All the fight goes out of Cruz in a gust of relief. He sags onto his pillow, his eyes closing as he palms his heart.

When he rolls over to turn off the lamp, I know I should speak up. I should tell him I'm afraid of the dark, but the kiss was too beautiful, the moment perfect. I don't want to ruin it by being childish.

My skin goes cold the second I'm doused in darkness. I am too afraid to say anything. I don't want to be the baby who's afraid of the monsters that lurk in the shadows, but that's exactly what I am. My body locks down completely, even as I'm sandwiched by unfettered love and warmth on both sides.

I'm safe, I remind myself, though the pep talk doesn't do much good. My muscles are on full alert. Before I know it, my body is trembling.

Santos cups my elbow and rubs up the length of my

arm. I can feel his confusion in the study of my body. Nothing goes unnoticed with him.

"Adelita, are you cold? What's wrong? You're shivering."

I can't answer. I can't move. The dark is oppressive, pushing down on my chest like a many-ton weight I will never be able to stand up against.

This is PTSD, my educated brain says, quite unhelpfully.

Santos sits up and runs to the door, flicking on the light.

Just like that, my demons are vanquished. Of course Santos would find a way to set me free without even knowing the enemy.

Cruz sits me up. Even though his body isn't as strong and agile as either of us are used to, I'm a doll in his arms as he holds me to his chest. "What just happened?" He shakes his head at himself. "I knew it was too far. I shouldn't have kissed you. I'm sorry, Addy. I messed it all up. I knew that whichever moment I chose, it would be the wrong one. But that was the really wrong one."

I squeeze his bicep as life floods back into my lungs. "No, Cruz. The kiss was perfect. It's me. I'm the one who's messed up." I scrub at my eyes as Santos comes back to sit beside us on the bed. "This is embarrassing.

Let's just go back to sleep. We can talk about it all in the morning."

That's a lie. The second I say it, I feel the sour notes on my tongue. I don't want to talk about this. I don't want to talk about any of it. Daylight won't change that.

Santos envelops my hand between his, earnest compassion filling his face. "*Corazón*, what is it?"

I press my lips together and shake my head. "I was just being a baby. I'm keeping you both awake. I don't want to do that. You need to sleep."

Santos has an unquenchable desire to give me whatever I want. What I really want is to not talk about this, so he folds easily, thank goodness.

Cruz, on the other hand, doesn't give a crap about what I want. He cradles my torso with one arm, and with his other hand, pinches my chin between his thumb and forefinger. When he angles my face up to stare into his hardened expression, my stubborn pride begins to whither under his glare. He commands with one word, but it's all he needs to say to get me going. "Talk."

I hate that I obey. "I don't like the dark. We can talk about why later. Much later. But for tonight, can we sleep with the lamp on?"

Cruz doesn't let go of my face, but tilts me upward, so he can meet my lips with a searing kiss. "Was that really so hard?"

"Yes."

He snorts as he lays me back down, but Santos is already on his feet. He disappears into the hallway and returns a minute later with something he plugs into the wall. "Nightlight," he explains. "Cruz won't be able to get decent rest with the lamp on. Will this work?" He flicks off the overhead light to test the strength of the tiny bulb glowing in the socket.

My shoulders deflate. "That's perfect. Thank you."

Santos crawls into the bed and then up my body, caging me in with his four limbs. "Why you ever hesitate to tell me what you need, I'll never know."

"She's prideful," Cruz comments.

"You're one to talk," I grouse.

Cruz grumbles, but lays down beside me while Santos kisses my lips with a gentlemanly softness. It makes me question how anyone could call him a savage.

"Sleep," Santos urges us both, leaning over me to kiss Cruz's cheek.

We have the hugest bed I've ever seen, but we hardly need the space. The three of us tangle together, indulging in the feel of protecting each other, and of being protected. Santos' arm hangs over my stomach, his knees angled to match the curve of mine. Cruz buries his nose in my neck and hooks my leg over his, so his knee can slip between my thighs. His lips kiss the tender spot in the crook of my neck, coiling me with need he has no intention of satiating.

I love having them this close. Without purposefully coordinating, Santos kisses one of my shoulders at the same time Cruz kisses the other.

A shiver rocks through me, only this time, there's no trace of the fear I felt in the darkness.

15

CATCHING UP

CRUZ

Waking from a sex dream is infinitely better than waking from the torments of La Sayona. Adelita's shapely legs stay threaded through mine as I blink the room into focus. Rousing to find a sexy woman wrapped around me is just about the best alarm clock in the world. Her breasts are covered in lace, begging to be nipped at through the thin material. Her robe slipped from her shoulders in the night, revealing brownish-copper skin that draws me in like nothing else.

I've been trying so hard not to be attracted to her. I want nothing but the best for Santos, and worried I might be taking it from him if I gave in to my infatuation with this *belleza*. But now that we're here in this strange dance of a relationship I never thought possible, parts of me that have always felt out of sync are now strangely calm.

My body aches from head to toe. My joints are stiff and sore. Maybe Santos shouldn't have locked the healer out, because I'm feeling the effects of dehydration now.

Still, uninterrupted sleep for who knows how many hours has been bliss.

Judging by the light that filters through the crack under the door, I can tell it is well past dawn.

Santos is dead to the world, his cheek smooshed against the back of Addy's head while he holds her in slumber.

I roll away as deftly as I can, putting my feet on the floor as I pad toward my dresser. I pull on clean gym shorts and leave the room as quietly as I can, hoping not to wake them.

Rafi greets me as I enter the kitchen. He's sitting atop the counter, much like we did when we were little, begging Aarón to teach us how to play with knives. Rafi is halfway through a bowl of oatmeal, and nods when he sees me. "Morning. The healer's going to kick your teeth in when she sees you. Fair warning."

I chuckle as I pour myself a glass of water and down it in a few constrictive gulps. Then I pull down three bowls. "Santos locked her out last night."

Rafi takes another bite, keeping his eyes on my movements as I ladle out the oatmeal from the pot into the bowls. "You sleep alright, Cruz?"

It's an innocent-sounding question, but it's ripe with meaning. "Slept like a baby, tucked in the arms of an angel."

I cringe at my poetic words. I never sound this sappy.

Rafi's mouth drops open. "Whoa. That's deep."

I chuckle at myself. "Honestly, I can't help it. There's no use in being stalwart or distant anymore. Adelita let me kiss her. I'll be her fluffy bunny coated in sugar, if that's what she wants."

Rafi snorts into his oatmeal. "Ho, man. You've got it bad. Did you really just say that? I mean, good for you, but yikes. That's a tall leap you're taking." He keeps his eyes on his bowl. "Santos is okay with you kissing his girl?"

I nod, grateful I covered this base. "We're all on the same page."

Rafi grants me half a smile and a fist bump. "Finally. Good for you, man. Good for all three of you."

Aarón shuffles into the kitchen and stops short upon seeing me. His eyebrows shoot upward, and suddenly his wiry frame turns formidable. "I'd like to know who told you to get out of bed, young man. You're on the mend, which means you don't get up to make breakfast.

I'll bring it to you, and I don't want to hear another word about it."

I hold up my hands with a sheepish grin. "Sorry, Aarón. Addy and Santos are still sleeping. I thought I'd get a jump on the day."

Aarón frowns at me. "The only thing you have on the schedule is drinking water and dealing with your healer, who couldn't be more irritated you all locked her out."

Consuela flits into the kitchen at the sound of Aarón's raised voice. "Cruz, are you alright? Did you sleep well?"

Rafi grins at me like he wants me to throw him to the ground, his eyebrows dancing. "He slept like a baby in the arms of an angel."

Consuela gapes at me, and I see the hope rising in her eyes. "You did? You're alright?"

I usually try not to see her concern for me. I don't need a mother. Never have. But the optimism in her eyes as they shimmer in my direction tugs at my stony heart. "I'm just fine."

She glides toward me in her teal dress that matches the backsplash of the kitchen. Consuela cups my face, examining the bags under my eyes. For once, I don't pull away. "I'm so glad to hear that. I was worried."

Jeez. Poor thing. She shouldn't care this much. It'll

give her an ulcer. "You never need to worry about me, Mom. I'm always fine."

I don't know why I called her that. Maybe because I know she needs to hear it. I've always kept it from her. I've always addressed her by her first name, but even that hard shell has been cracked away.

Consuela freezes, her lips parting in shock. I've finally learned respect and manners all in one day. I guess that is worth gaping at.

Consuela comes to life and throws her arms around my neck, her tall frame quaking as tears dot my neck.

I knew this would happen. She wears her emotions like raw nerves for anyone to poke at. Calling her Mom is such a small thing.

A small voice chimes in my conscience: *Then why did I hold it from her for all these years?* It's all she wanted from me, and I deprived her of it just so I could keep my distance. Let her know she didn't have a hold on me.

I'm an ass.

One arm finds its way around her, patting awkwardly because I really only know how to hug Rafi, Santos and Adelita.

"I'm sorry," I mumble, apologizing for a great number of things. For holding back from her. For being terrible at hugging. For looking the other way when she walks into a room. For...

...for thinking that asserting dominance was more important than letting her be herself in her own home.

When Consuela finally pulls away, her face is dotted with tears and her cheeks are a splotchy red. "What can I do, *hijo*? Anything you need."

She's so poised all the time. I've never cared about things like that. But now, maybe I do. Maybe I want to learn how to eat like a composed man who belongs at a table beside Addy. Consuela can help me with that.

I really wish Rafi wasn't watching me right now.

I clear my throat, ducking my head. "Later on, maybe you can help me not to look like an idiot around Adelita. You're always sitting so straight at the table and doing things properly. I should probably learn how to not embarrass myself in front of her."

I have no idea why this elicits more tears from her, but now they're streaming. Consuela nods emphatically. "Of course, *hijo*. Let me go fetch the healer for you." Then she turns and bolts out of the kitchen.

I rub the nape of my neck. "Jeez. Did I say something wrong?"

Rafi looks just as stunned. "No. Not wrong. You said something right, which is like, really weird. You just grew a new personality that all of a sudden has manners. It's like you sprouted a second head."

I roll my eyes at Rafi. "Hilarious."

"More water," Aarón urges, pressing a glass into my grip. "And go lay down. I'll bring you breakfast."

I set the three bowls on a tray, along with three spoons. "Already done."

Aarón grumbles in my direction, but I don't care. I want to be the one to take care of them. It's been too long since Santos or I have eaten anything substantial, and I have no idea the status of Adelita's health.

Dad refused to tell me anything about her abduction, except that Tavita was being controlled and has been granted clemency.

I have a million questions, but figure I should start with offering breakfast.

Rafi tags along with his own bowl. "If you're all going to be doing a rehash, I want in. Don't go edging me out of the important stuff because you three have your funky groove going on. I kissed her first, so I'm in this."

I narrow my eyes at him when we reach the door. "Fine, but you have to stop saying things like 'funky groove.' And wait until I wake them up. Actually, can you get a pitcher of water? Santos is dehydrated."

"So are you, Cruz. Don't forget that. One of these days, you need to actually rest. I'd choose today, if I were you. There's a hot woman in your bed. That's an excuse for a day of rest that doesn't require an illness."

I kick at Rafi to get him away from the door, and enter with the tray.

Adelita is stunning. Midnight hair curling around Santos' bicep, her hand stretched atop the spot where I was. Even in sleep, she reaches for me. I love that.

Falling for Adelita has been a swift descent. I thought I could brace myself forever, but now that I'm falling, I don't know why I resisted for so long. I don't care that I look like a sap with breakfast on a tray. It doesn't bother me one bit that she loves Santos. So long as she loves me, too, she can have whatever she wants.

Starting with water, because I know how to protect my family.

When I shut the door, it rouses Santos, whose arm shoots across Addy's body to shield her from whatever might attack.

We've been on the road for too long. We have no sense of how to be normal—how to hear a door and not assume it's the Kalku.

No more. There are other soldiers who can go out on missions. It doesn't always have to be us.

Santos rubs his eyes and sits up, though he keeps one hand on Addy at all times. "Morning."

The sound of his voice is still jarring. At least five times a day, it shocks me all over again that my brother finally has his voice.

Adelita stretches her arm over her head. I swear, my mouth waters when her breast tilts and nearly pops out of her nightgown. That thin piece of lace teases me like nothing else.

She yawns and sits up beside Santos, cuddling into his side. "Morning, Cruz."

I swallow hard, hoping she didn't catch me staring. "I thought we could eat a little. It's been a while for Santos and me. And we locked out the healer last night, so we need to catch up on water intake. Then we can go back to sleep." I kick the door shut behind me and set the tray on the middle of the bed, taking care not to jostle the mattress as I climb in beside them.

I hand Adelita her bowl, and Santos, his. Then I relax, knowing they are taken care of. My back is tender from the beating I endured, but I still recline against the headboard while I shovel spoonfuls into my mouth.

There's a shadowed spot around her eye, like she slept with makeup on or something.

"Your back is hurting you," Adelita comments with a frown. "I can heal your cuts, you know. I didn't offer last night because you needed sleep more than anything else. But if you want, I can fix it today." She taps her lips, reminding me of her kisses that heal abrasions.

"Nah." I take a chance and lean over to press my lips to hers, testing to see if her affection for me holds in the daylight. It's not a ravishing, but a clear declaration that our connection should happen at all hours of the day.

She doesn't pull away. In fact, miracle of miracles, she leans in, sighing contentedly and stroking my cheek with her delicate fingertips. "Are you sure? I don't like you in pain."

"My little softy. They'll heal alright on their own. I'm still a little out of sorts. Don't think I could handle the deep cleaning your kisses can do."

Her shoulders relax as we share another easy kiss. "Thanks for breakfast. Did you sleep alright?"

My eyebrows waggle mischievously when a replay of her straddling me floods my mind's eye. "Had some very good dreams."

She blushes, and I can't help but be drawn to the sight. I touch her cheek, loving the way her skin heats my finger. I don't feel the need to look away when she kisses Santos. For reasons I can't quantify, the sight settles my insides.

Santos situates the covers over her lap and his, constantly tending to her.

When Rafi comes in with a water pitcher, Adelita grins up at him. "I hear you're quite the hero. You got everyone home safely."

Rafi leans over me to kiss her cheek, and then sneaks a bite off her spoon. "Tell me I'm amazing."

"You're amazing, Rafael. I'm glad you're back. Are you feeling alright?"

"Never better. All I did was flex my bicep, and the Kalku fainted. Easiest battle ever." Rafi sits at the foot of the bed, crossing his legs. "Any word on when we get our next assignment?"

When the next words tumble out of my mouth, everyone stills. "We're staying put for a while. A few weeks. Maybe a month or more."

No one speaks; they all stare at me as if I've gone insane.

Maybe I have. I'm okay with that.

Rafi finally breaks the silence. "What do you know that I don't? Since when do we take weeks off?"

I motion around the bedroom. "Since all four of us are broken. Máximo found a way to snatch one of us out of our bed. In our home. We can be useful here. It's time to hand the baton to someone else. Let them go out on missions for weeks at a time."

Santos gapes at me. Adelita engages in that consummate studying face she wears when she's processing without showing her cards.

Rafi is the only one who finds words. "But you love being on the road."

I shrug. "Maybe I don't want to run anymore. Maybe I want to stay put for once." I pour a glass of water for

Santos and then one for Adelita, making sure they drink enough. While they sip, I steer the conversation in a new direction. "I want to know what happened while we were separated. We need to see this thing from all angles."

Santos frowns in her direction. "Starting with where you got that black eye."

My spine stiffens. "That's what that is?"

Adelita waves off our concern. "It's barely there anymore. It's fine."

Rafi loses his jocularity, his face turning stony. "What happened?"

Adelita takes an uncommonly long time drinking her water. I do nothing to fill the silence because I'm not about to let her off the hook. I want answers. She's hiding something, and it's going to gnaw at me until I hear every bit of it.

When she hands me the empty cup, she makes to crawl out from between Santos and me. "I need to shower."

I grab onto her hips and tug her back to my side. Thank goodness she doesn't wriggle from my grip; I'm too weak to do much. "Not so fast. I know what happened with Rafi and Santos. I was with them. I want to know what happened with you."

"Your dad can probably tell you that stuff. Nothing too crazy. I'm here, aren't I?"

She swallows hard through her blatant lie, so I know it's going to be bad. I brace myself for her story, refusing to back down. "Talk."

But this time, my forcefulness only succeeds in shutting her mouth more firmly.

Eva was right; I have no idea how to speak to women.

Santos comes to my aid, threading his fingers through hers. "Dad told us that Tavita was under Máximo's control. He said that she poisoned the three of us with our steamed milk that night. I don't remember you being taken at all. I just woke up with a bad headache, and you were gone. It was terrible. I tore through the village, tracking your scent on four legs as best I could, but you were gone." He mimes stabbing himself in the stomach. "Where did she take you?"

Of course it's Santos who gets her to talk. I need to get better at this. I'm great with knives. Bad with people.

Adelita fiddles with the tie on her bathrobe, staring at it instead of looking at us. "Máximo put a listening device in Tavita's head. Sewed it in behind her ear. It's why she refused to speak to anyone for so long. She didn't want Máximo overhearing. Another fun thing Máximo can do is sacrifice a person, which gives him enough magical mojo to control her body. Tavita was shocked when she saw Santos, and spoke aloud. I guess that's how Máximo found out I was here. He must've sacrificed someone that night so he could force her hand to abduct me. He takes over her body and makes her do what he wants."

"I saw her," I rasp. Rafi hands me a glass of water. "In my dream, there were two of you. I didn't realize I was seeing you and Tavita. Then when you were gone, La Sayona came into my mind."

Adelita flinches, as if the mere mention of my tormentor pains her. I love her tender heart. "Tavita took me away. The second she could, she helped get the poison out of me. Eventually I got the whole story from her, and we worked together from there. But the Kalku found us."

My eyes close. That's what Dad wasn't telling us. We got the bare bones of the story. Granted, we were barely upright when we got home, but still. If Addy gets taken by the Kalku, I want to know about it.

"How did the slaughter go?" Rafi asks casually. "I'm picturing you going to town and killing them all in a minute flat."

The silence that greets us is damning. My stomach drops as Adelita lowers her chin. "I'd been poisoned. I was barely upright. I couldn't fight off a mosquito. They captured us easily and took us to their cave."

A wave of nausea hits me afresh.

The information is too much for Santos. He slips out of the bed, standing with his back to the wall. His fists clench while a muscle in his jaw jumps. I never noticed he does that, but now that his hair is short, I can see the details more clearly.

She chews on her lower lip, glancing at Rafi as if silently asking him to intervene, to make it so she doesn't have to tell the rest of the story.

But Rafi doesn't let her off the hook. Instead, he takes Santos' spot beside her, massaging her nape and offering his body as a pillow she can rest against.

Why didn't I think of that?

"You must have been terrified."

She nods, cuddling into his side like a little girl. She looks tiny, curled up in his arms. "They wanted to hold us until Máximo gave them their next orders of where to take us. They injected Tavita with something that knocked her out, and then they lowered us into a pit. More like an abandoned well or something inside of their cave. It was stories deep, and pitch black." Her eyes flick to the wall. "So the nightlight helps. Thanks for getting that, Santos."

Santos doesn't acknowledge the gratitude. The only

emotion in his eyes is pure murder. He's beyond words, so Rafi coaxes Adelita on. "Did they hurt you?"

"I was too weak from all the puking to fight, so they didn't do more than knock me around a bit. We were in the pit for a day or two. I'm not sure. Time is kind of fuzzy. They starved us. Tavita was knocked out the entire time. It was freezing down there. I thought she might die of frostbite, if starvation or the drugs they gave her didn't take her out first."

Santos starts banging the back of his head against the wall.

"Tio Bruno found us. Him and a bunch of soldiers. They set the cave slave free, so that's good. His name is David. He removed Máximo's device from Tavita, so we won't go through that ever again. She's still on the mend. Tio Bruno is taking care of her."

When the banging starts to worry me, I'm out of the bed and standing in front of Santos, putting myself in his line of vision. "Listen to me, Santos. The Kalku have been dealt with. They will not take her ever again." Over my shoulder, I ask Adelita, "Did Tio Bruno leave anyone alive?"

"Only David. He'd been enslaved with them for a year, so he was taken back to his family."

"Hear that?" I ask Santos, holding his head still so he can't knock it against the wall anymore. "They won't come for her ever again. They're all dead. No one is taking this life away from you. See me? I'm right here. See Rafi? You're never getting rid of his ugly mug."

Rafi crosses his eyes. "Hey!"

I wrap Santos in a hug, as I always do when he's on the verge of digressing. My grip needs to be stronger to center him, but this is the best I can do. "Adelita is in our bed, in our home, safe from the Kalku. We're taking a long break, Brother. She's going to rest and have the best life anyone's ever dreamed. No one will take her from you ever again." I kiss his cheek, hoping it grounds him.

Santos loosens his fists and finally wraps his arms around me. "They took her from my arms. Máximo has my brother, Cruz. He has Santiago! I cannot let him be lost over there. I need to get him back." He shakes his head into my shoulder. "But I can't leave her side!"

I pull back just enough so I can get in his vision and grip his shoulders. "Listen to me. We're going to take this time off in the village and make a plan. No way are we letting Máximo keep Santiago. He's your twin, which means he's my brother, too. Do you think I let people tear apart my family like that?"

Santos sniffs and shakes his head.

"That's right. We'll figure this out. We just need to think it all through so we don't make any mistakes.

We've got Tavita, who's been there. She can help us plan out the best way to sneak out Santiago."

"You've got me," Adelita pipes in. "Once I'm on my feet again, I can help get him back for you."

All three of us answer as one. "Not a chance."

Then Rafi explains. "Máximo already tried abducting you. There's no way you're going to set foot on his island. You'll stay here."

Her face sours, and I can tell this is going to be the start of a long argument. "Enjoy that delusion. Santiago is my boyfriend's brother. I'm not going to just sit around and drink tea while he's being mistreated. I'm useful. You know you'll need my muscle for protection."

My teeth grind as I lock eyes with her. "I don't have the patience for this conversation right now. If Tio Bruno will let you on the island, I will consider it. Until you convince him, it's a moot point."

Never going to happen. Tio Bruno doesn't trust a soldier he hasn't trained himself, so he'll never agree to it.

Adelita is mollified for the time being, which lets me off the hook.

But I see the determination in her gaze. Adelita won't stay behind without a fight.

IT MATTERS HOW I GET THERE
ADELITA

I keep my focus at the forefront of my mind, even as sweat drips down the back of my neck.

Tio Bruno's bark always has a vicious bite to it. "That was slow. You're getting worse at this, not better. Is that what you meant to have done?"

I tuck my attitude away, though I have plenty to say to the man who is never pleased with anything.

I need Tio Bruno's seal of approval if I'm to be given the green light to go to the island to help liberate Santiago. The only problem is that Tio Bruno is an insufferable donkey, and I'm this close to punching his lights out, which would severely limit his chances of giving me a thumbs up.

Though, it would be satisfying.

Tio Bruno gave me chainmail gloves, which definitely help. My muscles are strong, but my skin can tear if I'm not careful. Given that I have to flip this stinking car from one end of the field to the other, there are precious few options for being careful.

Tio Bruno times each full rotation the car makes, marking my fatigue, and I'm guessing my attitude, as well. He's a jerk.

"Strength means nothing if you have no endurance," Tio Bruno chides. Loudly. Every time, it's like his volume grows. It's embarrassing to be told you suck in so many different ways while your boyfriends, sister and surrogate family watch like it's a movie all made for entertainment.

Except for Santos, who looks like he might vomit.

My mother's words echo into my brain over and over: "It matters how you get there."

It matters if I get to the island by sacrificing the good parts of my personality to spite.

I tip the car over onto its head, and then shove my weight under the lip of the rocking hood to give it another thrust. This one doesn't turn it all the way over, but it gives me enough leverage to right the dilapidated car on the second push.

I straighten myself with a gust of pride. It's the fifteenth time I've flipped this car, but each time feels like a victory. I never knew I could do this until Tio Bruno set up the exercise for me after his usual calisthenics didn't do much to push me.

Tio Bruno grunts at his timer. "You're listening to your pride. The Kalku will not be impressed if you can overcome one obstacle. You don't stop and celebrate until the job is done. That car needs to be past the opposite goal post. Then you get to breathe and congratulate yourself for taking your sweet time."

I glare at him. "Has anyone ever told you that they hate you?"

"It matters how you get there." My mother's credo vibrates through my tightened forearms. She would be confused to see me speaking like this—trying to take someone down rather than building them up.

Tio Bruno crooks an eyebrow at me. "Feelings are a waste of breath. You'll need every bit of yours to make it across this field, so I'd save your anger for someone who cares."

"You have issues," I grunt as I attack the car once more, tipping it onto its side. "I would say it's younger child syndrome. José is the leader of the Cáceres and you missed out by default. But you don't seem to resent your brother for his role." I give the car another push, toppling it on its head. "I could guess that you have some repressed sexuality issues, but Tavita hasn't complained yet, so I guess I'll have to wait and see if that's it."

I'm being mean. I'm using my education against him.

To be fair, he started it.

"Máximo gave the wrong person this gift. In the hands of a true warrior, it could mean absolute victory. In your hands? I'm embarrassed for you."

There are so many things I want to spout back at him, but I'm too winded for words.

When I say nothing, but keep on working, Tio Bruno prods at my tender spots again. "You were trained to be a cleaning lady, and it shows. Perhaps I should have you shining the shoes of the real soldiers."

It's a well-aimed hit to the gut, and I despise him for it.

When I collapse to my knees to take a breath, he kneels beside me. His voice is a low seethe meant to slice through my resolve. "Your mother raised you to be slaughtered. You are weak."

I have two choices: I can finish the assignment and keep rolling the car, or I can clock this jaggoff, and knock him out with a single punch.

I get to my feet and grip the lip of the car's frame. Ignoring him might be my best bet.

Or needling him the second I can catch my breath.

I keep rolling the car, throwing out hypotheses I

would never voice to a client during a session. If he wants to break me down, I'm taking him with me. I'm fueled by anger and resentment, not pride or the will to be better.

This is no way to train a soldier.

Halfway down the field, I stop completely. I'm exhausted, sure, but I'm emotionally spent. My short gym shorts cling to me in uncomfortable places. I shucked my t-shirt a while ago, and have been muscling through in my sports bra, which is also soaked with sweat.

I right myself, meeting Tio Bruno's eyes with venom that didn't exist before today.

If it truly matters how I get there, then I'm about to take the low road.

My voice carries with it a low boil that breaks across the field without me having to shout. "If I had to put money on the reason why you are the awful way you are, it's that you're a dinosaur. You're a dying breed of soldier who failed to evolve. You're afraid of being replaced, but you know it's time. So you take it out on anyone who dares surprise you, which is what you've been doing to me all day." I clench my fists through my snarl. "Do you feel like a big man now?"

I've hit his underbelly, and though part of me wants to sneer in victory at the sick look that twists his face, the other part of me knows I took this thing too far. There's no win when someone is crushed. That's not what my degree was for. Vengeance is not what my mom sacrificed so much to give me.

He responds by jerking toward me, like he's going to attack. He doesn't, but it's enough to spook me backwards, so I fall awkwardly on my butt. Then he stands over me, proving that yes, he does think of himself as a big man.

I don't expect him to reach out his hand to help me up, and for a second, I consider it might be a trick. When he hoists me up, he holds me in place. "You will never be truly great until you believe that there is nothing that can defeat you. Every time you attack that car, I see fear in your face. No matter how many times you flip it, you're afraid that you can't."

"Wrong," I admit, my voice choked. "I'm afraid that I can." Only I don't realize my deep-rooted fear until it spills out. My mouth twists.

Why would I be afraid of strength? That makes no sense.

Then the deeper truth fights its way to the surface. "I don't want to be my father's daughter."

Tio Bruno's eyebrows raise, but he doesn't argue with my feelings, for which he gets a gold star. "Fear is no reason to move forward. It is no reason to cross an ocean to get to the island. Certainty is the only motivator that matters. *Know* that you can roll this car. *Know* that your strength surpasses your enemy's." He meets my eyes without a touch of aggravation. Finally, he's teaching me something valuable in a way I can hear it. "Know that you are worthy of the gifts you were given. You've taken a madman's blessing and hid it from the world until you best understood how to use it. You will turn that weapon against him before this is all finished." Then he squeezes my hand. "Worthy."

He cups my shoulder, holding me in place until his words sink in.

"I don't want to be his," I whisper. "What does it say about me that I can do this? It makes me like Máximo. It makes his gift useful for me. How dirty will that make my hands? Will I turn out like him?"

Tio Bruno takes two fingers and taps them under my chin. "That's fear talking again. You won't get anywhere with that. Fear holds you in place. Fear drowns you where you stand. *Know*, Adelita. Know that you will never become Máximo because your motivations have nothing to do with his. You want to keep your family safe. He wants to exploit his. You are not his daughter." The corner of his mouth flicks up for just a breath. "You'll turn out like me before you ever turn out like him."

That little nugget shocks us both.

He musses my hair and then steps back, checking his timer. "Don't set your sights on defying him. Don't think twice about pleasing me." He cuts the flat of his hand across the center of his body. "Protect your family. That's all you need to do right now." His voice carries with it the weight of a command. "Can you finish the job, soldier?"

I'm honestly not totally sure, but then I remember Tio Bruno's heart-to-stony-heart: I cannot let fear inside. I have to know I can do this.

So I grip the lower lip of the car and start flipping. I save my grunts and frustrations, because I know I can do this. I can protect my family. I can go to the island and free Santiago. I'm not going to lose this battle. I will use my father's gift in ways he couldn't comprehend—which, when you think about it, is what happens with all traits that parents pass down.

My father's plans for me are nothing compared to the plans I have for myself.

Flipping a car is hard, but harder would be staying behind and waiting for my family to come home. Impossible would be doing nothing while sending people to fight a battle I know I can win.

Because if I can flip a car across a football field, there's no fight I cannot win.

My face is dead as I work, my feet grounded and my body tight. There is no one in my periphery because my entire focus is on my family. I will protect them. I will keep the tribe safe from Máximo.

There is no fear now, only certainty. No malice, only love.

Tio Bruno pushed me past my rage so I could find my gentleness, which is where my most potent muscle lies.

Mom was right: it matters how you get there. I don't want our road to victory to be paved with second-guessing myself and worries that I'll become someone I was never destined to be.

I will look after my family. After all, I am my mother's daughter.

I work tirelessly without pause, ignoring praise and casting aside any snide judgments. It's not about their approval; it's about keeping them safe.

I don't hear any of it until Santos rushes to my side, waving his hands. "Stop. Adelita, you're well past the goal post. If you keep going, you'll hit the wall."

My arms pause their lift, and I lower the car to the grass. I look around, and sure enough, the goalposts are several meters behind me.

Tio Bruno watches me to gauge my reaction, which I refuse to give him. Instead, I march over to him with a stern expression. "What's my next test? I'm ready for it."

His mouth pulls to the side, hiding his amusement. It mingles with praise he won't verbalize. "That was far and away your best time. You sure you don't want a break?"

"Will a break show you I'm the best one to go over there and take out Máximo?"

Tio Bruno claps me on the shoulder again. "Very good. We'll go to the training grounds for the next part. Strength won't do you much good there."

My steeled confidence drops, but I hold my composure, hoping the next test won't be as difficult as the first.

17

FIGHTING WITH MY FAMILY
SANTOS

I cannot watch, but I have to. I'm her healer. I need to know every spot on her that gets hit, no matter how much pain it causes me. There's a little "oo!" noise she makes whenever Tio Bruno gets in a shot, which is far too often for my liking.

Once is too often for my liking, but this is overkill. It's like he's trying to make her quit.

She has no formal training. Cruz said he would train her, but he didn't do more than a few rounds before he realized he doesn't have the stomach for inflicting pain on our woman.

Tio Bruno has no such qualms. They are sparring using wooden daggers with blunt edges, which sometimes inflict more damage than the real kind. He knows how to pop the weapon out of her hand a hundred different ways, and demonstrates them all on her.

Tavita watches by my side, and for the most part, we wince in unison every time Adelita takes a hit. She's not too bad, Adelita's sister. We've all been taking our time getting a feel for each other. Her clear devotion to Adelita eases any of the lingering tension that could have driven a wedge between us all.

"I hate this," Tavita admits. "I mean, I get that this is important for her to learn, but my heart stutters when she stubs her toe."

I chuckle, because I know exactly how she feels.

I gauge my temper by the frustration in Adelita's eyes. She's not afraid of the blows. She's hurt by them, sure, but she's more angry she's being so easily bested. Her nostrils flare and her teeth grind as she swings wildly.

Tavita's face is stern as she watches the two knock each other around. "Hot bath tonight. She's going to be sore. Hot bath and a massage. Can you manage that?"

I nod once. "Of course. She might be too sore to be touched, though."

"True. Then at least make sure she gets a good night's sleep after her bath."

"Yes, Ma'am."

Tio Bruno pauses to catch his breath, glancing Tavita's way. News of their relationship didn't take long to surface, though no one is brave enough to tease them about it—except for Adelita. Usually there's no apology touching Tio Bruno's tongue, but his sheepish expression when he regards his new girlfriend reveals the soft marshmallow no one knew was inside the hardened military leader. "Tavita, why don't you go get yourself some dinner. You don't want to see this."

Tavita folds her arms over her chest. "I'm good where I'm at."

Tio Bruno hangs his head. "This is all standard for a new soldier. I need to see how capable they are when they come to me. Then I know how to train them."

Tavita grants him a breezy smile that holds no joy. "You're very good at your job. I'll stay parked here, though. See, I never got to be with my sister when the bully on the playground beat her up."

Tio Bruno's shoulders droop while Cruz sniggers. "Jeez. I'm not..." But he can't claim he's not a bully. He's many things, but Tio Bruno is not a liar.

Tio Bruno tosses his wooden knife to the ground and stretches his arms over his head.

Adelita takes a drink from the water bottle Cruz has ready for her. Usually there isn't an audience for these kinds of entrance exams, but Cruz and I won't let Adelita out of our sight.

Rafael hovers just as much, solidifying our team with sarcasm. "I'm thinking she'll only have two dozen bruises in the morning. Twenty-five is such a nice, round number. Frankly, I'm disappointed I didn't get my money's worth."

Tio Bruno runs his hand over his face. "Rafi, she's useless with a knife. Our best bet is to teach her how to escape holds, because they're definitely going to capture her." He motions to Adelita, who is sweating and holding her arm. "Go ahead and put Rafi in a hold, Cruz. The two of you can demonstrate how to get out."

Rafi grins through the whole thing, loving that he gets permission to throw Cruz over his body and slam him on the ground.

We've practiced these moves so many times, it's like child's play. They're important to learn, but once you get the muscle memory down, there's not much to it.

Over and over, they demonstrate for Adelita, who grimaces every time Cruz hits the ground. The sun shines overhead, as it's done every day since Cruz kissed Adelita. Eventually we might have to go on a road trip just so nature can give the crops a little rain. We're not used to his pleasant moods.

"Good," Tio Bruno says. "You can try it now. Do you understand the mechanics?"

Adelita nods, but I can see there's no conviction to it.

She's nervous. She's been snatched at too many times for a play abduction not to be triggering.

She taught me what that word meant, and I can see it all over her face.

I cross the grass between us, ignoring Tio Bruno's scowl as I cup her face. "We can take a break, *Corazón*. I can tell this is too much."

Tio Bruno chimes in with an ever-so-helpful, "It's too much if she gets stolen again. She's a target, so she needs to learn how to get out of holds. It can't always be about strength. That's one weapon. You need several if you're going to win."

He's right, but I despise him for it.

Adelita nods, braving her way through her fear. She gives off a look of determination that nothing will be too much for her.

It breaks my heart. I don't want my sweet Adelita to be turned into a soldier. I love the soft things about her, and don't wish her to harden her gentler parts for survival's sake. I'm not protecting her well when I see her sweetness fading to the tune of readiness and war.

Instead of Rafi, whom I trust with Adelita, Tio Bruno comes up behind her, ripping her from my hands and jerking her body backward against his chest. His forearm chokes around her throat as he backs her up, stealing her steadiness so she can't even salvage her footing.

Breathe through it, I remind myself. *This is a drill. She's not in actual danger.*

I'm holding myself in place until a small noise of distress surfaces through her struggle.

Everything in me snaps, and I'm lost to my rage.

My knife comes out as I lunge for Tio Bruno, my teeth bared. I've never drawn a weapon on my commander before, but at the hint of her fear, I am a man unhinged.

Before I can slash at Tio Bruno's side to knock his arm loose, Cruz races past me, pummeling his own uncle from the side.

Shock comes second to Adelita's safety, but I still feel it. Cruz attacking Tio Bruno? Never thought I'd see the day.

Again.

The first time, Tio Bruno had drawn a knife. That made sense for Cruz to attack. But this is a drill.

I shouldn't have lunged, sure. But Cruz never loses his cool like this.

It's a tangle of limbs when I involve myself, ripping Adelita from Tio Bruno's surprised grip. I fling her behind my back, securing her arms around my waist so I can use my body as a human shield. "Hurt her again, and that will be the last thing you do."

Fat drops of rain fall down from above, pelting us out of nowhere. It was sunny a half a minute ago.

Cruz stands over his uncle. Though he's unarmed, it's clear he is ready to fight to the death if anything like that happens again.

I am not opposed to this.

"Whoa." Rafi's eyes are wide as he gapes at us. "Everyone, take a step back. Adelita, are you alright?"

She nods, her face moving the back of my shirt. But it's not enough to quell my angst. My wolf is in physical pain, thinking she might be scared or hurt. He's clawing at my ribs, howling to rectify this injustice.

Rafi seems to understand this, holding his arms out to still us all. "Tell them you're okay, or things are going to get real messy."

Her voice is squeaky. "I'm alright, guys. What just happened?"

Tio Bruno blinks up at us in confusion, as if Cruz and I are the ones who have lost our minds. He's just put his hands on Adelita, yet we're suspect for insanity? Nice. He holds his hands up in surrender as the rain pelts us, which is something I never thought I'd see. I've gone on raids with him where I thought for sure he would fall back—raids where he *should* have fallen back—but he took that as a challenge and charged harder. Tio Bruno is a mule of a man, stubborn to his core. Seeing him surrender so easily is more confusing than anything else.

It's even more perplexing than the knife in my hand, aimed at my commander. What... What am I doing?

I shake my head to clear it of the blind rage that was pulsing through me seconds ago. Adelita's fingers stroke up and down over the ridges of my abdomen, calming me enough to chase sense back into my brain. My knife lowers as my other hand covers hers across my stomach. "You are safe?"

She nods again into my back as Tavita inches toward us. "Adelita, let's go indoors, yeah? You'll catch cold if you stay out in this."

Thunder cracks, but I've been along on the ride through Cruz's tantrums enough times to know this is his doing. The storm inside of him can't confine itself anymore, so it manifests in the sky, soaking us through in seconds.

Cruz is frozen in place. I can feel the shock rolling off him in waves. "I attacked you," he says in disbelief to Tio Bruno. "You were... And I thought... And then I..."

Rafi maintains his position in the middle, his hands still outstretched to keep us all in place. "Put your knife away, Santos. Cruz, back up."

I glance down, surprised to find that I raised my dagger again without meaning to. It's pointing at Tio Bruno, threatening menace if he comes near Adelita again. I am a cave slave aiming a weapon at the army's commanding officer.

I truly have lost my mind.

Tavita and Rafi seem to be the only ones without terror striking their faces, so I go with their gentle lead. My knife sheaths itself as I lean into Adelita's embrace. Rain streaks down my face, marring my vision in spots, yet still I make out the worry in Tavita's eyes.

Worry, not surprise.

Adelita thumbs at my navel, letting me know she's okay, if not a little spooked, by what I'm quickly coming to understand was a complete and total overreaction on mine and Cruz's parts.

Cruz stumbles backward, staring at his hands as if he can't believe what they just did. Then his chin whips toward Adelita with trepidation marking the widening of his eyes.

Before anyone can say another word, Cruz turns on his heel and bolts away from us, running through the storm of his own making.

No matter how fast his feet carry him, he will not be able to outrun this.

18

SISTER SLUMBER PARTY
ADELITA

The second I shiver, Santos comes back to himself. The rain that came out of nowhere soaked me through minutes ago, but when Cruz bolted after attacking Tio Bruno, that's when I began to experience the sting of the cold.

"Inside," Santos suggests, turning to fix his palm to my back.

Tavita offers a hand to Tio Bruno, remaining with him to make sure he's alright.

Santos and I start walking toward home, but my feet feel leaden and clumsy. His hand on my back is usually a source of reassurance and calm, but his fingers quake just above the base of my spine. Whatever serenity I crave, I know I won't be able to draw from him.

We were going through defensive drills. Tio

Bruno was trying to teach me. I need to learn these things, otherwise the Kalku might get the drop on me. If the guys are going to go over and liberate Santiago, no way am I getting left in Cáceres. Tio Bruno had me from behind, but when I lost my balance, Cruz and Santos lost their minds. The shifting nature of our odd entanglement has reached a new level of strange, but this time, I'm not sure how to approach any of it.

I need... I'm not sure. I need a break. I need a shower. I need...

I need space.

As much as I know that's going to hurt Santos, I cannot tamp down my nature to serve his. That's not a relationship. I tell my clients all the time that if your partner can't value your needs, then he needs too much from you.

I have to trust that Santos values me, even when I'm out of sorts.

I stop partway to the house, letting the rain pelt me as thunder cracks so hard, it rattles my teeth.

Santos pauses beside me. "We should get inside. Cruz is an Acalica, remember? His moods are tied to the weather. He's worked up, so this storm isn't going to quell any time soon."

"I can't go home," I blurt out with no polish.

Santos turns to face me, his brows slamming down to pronounce his frown. "What do you mean?"

I shake my head and band my arms around my waist. "I need space. I need to spend some time in my brain alone. That was... I don't know what that was, and I need some time to think things through."

Santos wraps his arms around me, and instantly, I trust his strength. "Let's get you to your own bedroom, then. I'll sleep in mine, if you like. Is that enough space?"

My lower lip quivers. His unselfishness is something I never need to question. He can put my needs above his. I can trust our relationship. I can be broken and without answers, and it will be okay.

"I don't think so, but that was a good suggestion. I..." Then an idea pops into my mind that I instantly gravitate towards. "Could I stay the night with my sister?"

His body stiffens against the suggestion, his arms tightening around me. But when he speaks, his words come out gentle. "Of course, Adelita. She's your family. Come on, I'll walk you there and get you set up."

Relief floods my system as the rain assaults us with fat drops that fall harder than normal precipitation. The trail has quickly turned to slick mud, but Santos' arm bands around my back, holding onto me to make sure I don't slip. He's a good man, through and through.

Though there's nothing in it for him, he's walking me to the promise of sanity.

How I love this unselfish man.

We don't walk back toward the spot we were at, but beeline toward the edge of homes near the barracks, where Tavita has taken up residence. I haven't been in Tavita's home yet; she's only been there a week or so. But Santos knows her address and walks me there. His fist bangs on the door as he holds me tighter to his side.

When the door swings, both of our mouths fall open. "Tio Bruno? What are you doing here?"

It's sheer rudeness on my part, but Tio Bruno doesn't call me on it.

He doesn't answer me at all. Instead, he calls over his shoulder. "Tavita, your sister's here."

Tavita comes out in fuzzy pajama pants and an oversized sweatshirt, drying her hair with a towel. "Hey, honey-girl. You alright?"

Words desert me. I know I want to stay here, but I'm nervous to ask. I don't know her. Not really. Am I already the annoying little sister who needs too much and gloms on to her cooler older sibling?

Santos speaks when it's clear I'm freezing up. "Adelita's a bit shaken. She was wondering if she could stay with you tonight." He swallows hard. "I think I scared her."

I hate that he sees the truth through my hazy explanation. I'm not scared of him, exactly. I'm scared of the intensity of the three of us, of what it all means.

Tavita melts, sheer compassion radiating off of her. "You never have to ask. Get in here, girl."

Santos stands in the doorway gripping the jamb. I can tell he hates everything about this.

Tavita hugs my sopping form but addresses Santos. "I'll lock all the doors and windows. Bruno will stay here tonight to guard the house. Are you free for lunch tomorrow at noon? We can meet up with you, Rafael and Cruz then."

Somehow she knows the exact right thing to say to him. Santos' shoulders lower as he nods. "Thank you. Noon is good. Can I..." He looks nervous and a little ashamed. "Can I check your locks first? I want to make sure everything is secured before I go."

Tavita doesn't balk at the request. "That's a great idea. Bruno did a check already, but two sets of eyes are always appreciated. Do you want to see where Adelita will be sleeping?"

Santos nods, casting her a look of relief mixed with appreciation. "Yes. Thank you."

She's kind, even though Santos is being a bit ridiculous. We're in Cáceres, which is a safe place. Tio Bruno is here, so I can't imagine what idiot with a death wish might try to break in. Still, she escorts Santos around the house with incredible patience while I wait in the entryway with Tio Bruno.

"This is weird," I whisper to him.

He nods. "Weird is the only color that comes in. I've given up trying to understand why Santos does the things he does. The Kalku messed him up." Tio Bruno shrugs, as if that's the only explanation he requires. His eyes take on a note of insecurity, which looks odd on the towering hulk of a man. "Did I hurt you out there? Like, did I do actual damage?"

"Were the wooden knives supposed to tickle?" When he narrows his eyes at me, I wave him off. "I'm fine. Nothing's broken. You pissed me off a few times, but I can't imagine I'm the first person who's told you that." I pause for his amused snort. "We were doing escape drills. The guys overreacted, is all. I'm sorry it got all intense."

Tio Bruno gives me a look that says "what can you do?" but I can tell questions and concerns are brewing beneath the surface of his cool military exterior.

Tavita and Santos reappear, and amazingly, Santos is a modicum more relaxed, which I'm guessing is entirely Tavita's doing.

Without words, Santos scoops me with both arms, holding me to his chest with my feet hovering a few inches from the ground. "*Corazón*," he coos. "I will see you at noon. Do you need anything before I leave?"

I don't care that we're making a scene. "A kiss goodnight. That's all I need."

"Just one?" Santos teases. I'm so grateful there's sweetness in his voice.

His lips are soft, even though there's a current of panic beneath the tamed passion. Santos sucks on my lower lip, drawing my own unrest out of me so it doesn't settle too deep into my bones. I love the feel of his hard body against mine. Though we're both dripping and cold, none of that is as intense as the love I have for this great man.

When Santos sets my toes back on the hardwood floor, he nips my lips once more, and then brushes his nose across mine. "Keep the doors locked, yes?"

"Of course. I love you, Santos. Thank you for this."

He kisses my lips again. "I'm sorry I didn't control my temper out there." Then he turns his chin toward Tio Bruno. "Truly."

Tio Bruno nods once. "Goodnight, *sobrino*."

Santos goes to leave, but braces himself in the open doorway, as if each step away from me costs him a great effort.

When he finally leaves and shuts the door behind him, Tio Bruno moves to lock it. There are three different locks on the door. The top one is shiny and looks new.

A few seconds later, the handle jiggles from the outside. The corner of my mouth quirks. Santos is making sure the lock is in place before he leaves. I don't know why that strikes me as adorable, but it does.

Tio Bruno is less endeared to the man. He harrumphs with a scowl. "Like I don't know how to protect a home. Honestly."

Tavita exhales. "That went better than I expected. Good for him." She smirks at me. "He loves you, kiddo. And bonus: he's a good man. That combination is hard to find." She jerks her thumb over her shoulder when I sneeze. "Shower's all yours. I'll get you some dry clothes for the night, okay? Then when you get out, the three of us are going to have a long talk. There's more going on than either of you realize."

My heart sinks. "Please tell me it's something good. I cannot handle one more ounce of stress."

Tavita grimaces. "Shower. Then we'll talk."

I obey, shutting the bathroom door behind me and peeling off my clothes. There's something comforting about the beige walls and gray towels. The chief's house is gorgeous and lavish, but this place has no frills. It's kind of a relief. I could belong here. I don't have to know all the answers to live here for the night. These bare walls don't expect a thing from me.

The water is hot, and washes away the sting of the rain. Tavita's pajamas were big on her, and she's taller than I am, so I roll up the cuffs on the cozy flannel pants and tie the baggy shirt at the base of my spine.

When I emerge, Tio Bruno and Tavita are speaking in hushed, serious tones. They break off the conversation when they see me, but not before I hear my name.

Tio Bruno rubs the nape of his neck, and then moves past me to take his turn in the shower. He's carrying a bundle of clothes under his arm.

Has he slept here before? Does he keep spare clothes at Tavita's place?

My sister offers me a soft smile that chases away her earlier concern. "Come on. I ordered takeout, which should be here in twenty minutes. You want something to drink?"

"Only if it's strong," I admit.

She chuckles. "I don't blame you." Tavita takes a bottle of whiskey from the cabinet. "This strong enough?"

"It's perfect. Thanks."

She pours me a glass while I sit on a stool at the counter in her kitchen. This room as well has no frills, no "kiss the cook" decorations or anything to give it a lick of personality. Consuela's teal addiction makes their place explode with brightness and beauty, but here, there are no promises that life is happy. Just shelter, which is exactly what I need. Beige walls, gray dish towel, clean dishes in the drainer over the sink.

I take a drink and relish the burn as it grounds me. Tavita pours herself the same thing, and the two of us share a few minutes of silence, letting the evening settle before poking at the details of it all.

Finally, the right words find their way to the surface. "My life wasn't always this weird."

"Why would you say it's weird?" she jokes, and both of us giggle. Tavita sets down her tumbler and hefts herself up to sit atop the counter. She looks adorable poised like that. When Tio Bruno comes out in his pajamas, freshly showered, I can tell he's thinking the same thing.

"The three of us are going to have a talk," Tavita rules.

Instantly, my stomach tightens. "I came here to take a break from all of that. Could we put off the talk until tomorrow?"

Tavita won't be derailed. "Not really. Something might happen in the night, and I don't want you to be spooked if it does. I know things about you that I'm guessing you don't. When I learned the truth about myself, everything started to make a lot more sense. It was less overwhelming when I could see the full picture."

I pinch the bridge of my nose. "I don't have enough whiskey for this conversation. Not to sound like a brat, but how could you know things about me that I don't? We only just met last month."

Tavita motions to the cupboard, and Tio Bruno pulls down a tumbler for himself. Tavita tips the whiskey into his cup. When he takes his first sip, suddenly I feel as if we might all be on even footing. I'm not the kid in the room anymore. Tio Bruno's not the gruff authority figure. We're all just hanging out and having drinks together, rehashing about our weird lives.

"I know our father, Adelita. He explained things about my genetics. After that, a whole lot of questions I've always had finally made sense." Tavita takes a short sip of her drink, her gaze flicking to Tio Bruno. "I was planning on having this talk with you tonight, so it's just as well that Adelita is here. Two birds with one stone, I guess. I wasn't sure if she was like me in this way, but after tonight, there's no question."

Tio Bruno leans his butt against the counter, drink in hand. He looks so strange like this—dark gray pajama pants, white t-shirt stretched across his ridiculously massive chest. He looks so much like Cruz, only thicker around the ribs and with gray brushed through his black hair. The stern cut of his jaw makes him always look irate about something. Or maybe that's because his flawless bones structure never gives way to a smile.

Tavita's demeanor is usually no-nonsense and all bravery, but tonight, her shoulders go concave, and her gaze fixes on her tumbler. "When Máximo told me what I was, I didn't want to believe it. But it made too much sense not to. When I learned I had a sister, I hoped the magical genetic strain only landed in me. But after seeing Cruz and Santos lose their minds like that tonight, there's no question." Her eyes flick to me with silent apology, though I can't imagine what she has to be sorry for in all of this. "I'm La Ciguapa, and Adelita, so are you."

Though this means absolutely nothing to me, Tio Bruno gasps. He sets down his drink and shakes his head. "No. No, no. You can't be. La Ciguapa is a myth. It's not real."

Tavita meets his dread-filled gaze with humility shining in hers. "You know I'm right."

Tio Bruno inches out of the kitchen, shaking his head over and over. "No. That would mean I…"

I don't expect Tio Bruno to bolt out of the house in bare feet, running out into the storm, but that's exactly what he does.

Tavita slides off the counter and moves to shut the door behind him. Her steps are slow, her shoulders slumped. "Yeah, that's about what I expected he might do when he found out." Though her tone is nonchalant, her entire demeanor is crestfallen.

Judging by Tio Bruno's strong reaction, whatever La Ciguapa is, I can only hope I am not one.

19

LA CIGUAPA

ADELITA

*T*avita's feet shuffle slowly back into the kitchen after Tio Bruno's quick exit. "Well, there goes that. At least he got out early before things went too far."

I clutch my tumbler, examining the honey-colored drink through the glass. "Tavita, what are you talking about? I'm not from here. I'm from the regular world, where people say, 'huh?' if someone announces they're La See-Pow-Gua."

Tavita resumes her spot with her butt atop the counter, her legs crossed on the beige surface. "La Ciguapa. It's an old story the Kalku hold dear to. Why do you think they abduct women but never force them into their beds? They abduct children, rather than sire their own. They're afraid of women, Adelita, because they very much believe in La Ciguapa."

I set down my glass so I can massage my temples. "Please start further back than that. What is a Ciguapa? It must be bad if it strikes fear into the heart of Tio Bruno, who doesn't have a heart to begin with."

Tavita scolds me with a good-natured clucking of her tongue. "Bruno is a romantic."

I choke out a bitter laugh. "Maybe I should be the older sibling. You don't have your head on straight, if that's your judgment of that man."

Tavita doesn't take my sass to heart. "La Ciguapa is a woman who hypnotizes men. In Kalku lore, she can suck out their will with a kiss. The more they come together romantically, the more the man gives himself over to her until there's no trace of him left. He becomes a shell of a person, forfeiting the best parts of himself to be with her."

I can't keep the horror off my face. "Are you serious? That's awful! Talk about dysfunctional relationships."

"Yeah, well, we can't help who we are."

I gape at her. "I don't do that! I'm not sucking out Santos' or Cruz's souls."

But as soon as the words come out of my mouth, I question them. Santos did actually make the choice to give up his soul (at least, that's what he thought he was doing) when I asked him to take a picture with me. I was convinced Cruz didn't have a soul to begin with, but no man who kisses like he does can be accused of being dead inside.

Tavita is quiet while my thoughts play out on my features, my mouth drawing to the side.

"You don't mean to do it," she finally says in a quiet voice. The rain is falling hard outside, nearly drowning out her words. "Neither did I. When I learned what I was, I told myself I would never date again. Then I met Bruno. He's so unshakable that I thought he would be able to stand up against the parts of me I'm not all that proud of." She motions to the door, indicating his speedy exit. "I guess I was right. He got out before things got dark. Good for him."

She sounds sincere, but also unbearably sad that this is the turn her life has taken.

"Máximo is wrong," I seethe. "He's never even met me. He only knew you when you were in captivity. He would say anything to cut your confidence down to nothing."

Tavita takes a sip of her whiskey. "All those things are true, but Máximo is not wrong."

We sit in silence for a minute, both of us afraid to delve further into the muck.

When a knock bangs on the door, Tavita smirks and

hops down, flitting toward the entrance. "That's either my suitor or one of yours. Want to bet which one came back first?"

"I'm guessing it's the one without shoes."

Sure enough, Tio Bruno stomps into the entryway, standing like a brooding idiot as he drips on the welcome mat.

Tavita doesn't ask questions or look affronted. She merely pats his cheek twice, then moves to the bathroom and fetches a towel.

I can see the whole scene from my spot in the kitchen on my stool, though I should probably look away. But seeing Tio Bruno so out of sorts is a guilty pleasure of mine, I'm learning. I love that he has no idea what to do with his hands as Tavita scrubs the towel through his hair and then runs it over his arms. His whole body transitions from stiff to softening, back to brusque, and then leaning in to her touch when she helps him work his soaked shirt off.

Man, he's got a lot going on.

"I want the whole story. Everything. How you found out. How you confirmed it. La Ciguapa is a myth, Tavita."

She loops the towel over the doorknob, locks up again, and tugs his arm toward the kitchen. "Come on, big guy. I was just going to tell Adelita everything about it."

I'm not a fan of Tio Bruno shirtless, mainly because I don't want to know what a family member looks like half-naked. He's just as self-conscious, his arms crossing over his chest to fend off errant glances. "Talk."

Tavita bats her lashes at him. "Well, since you asked so nicely."

Tio Bruno doesn't back down, though I can tell he wants to.

Tavita hops back up onto the counter, crossing her legs. I wonder if she's ever sat on one of her own stools. "I was married for five years," she begins, surprising us both with a dive into the deep end. She keeps her gaze tethered to her drink. Her eyes go out of focus, like she's picturing a life that slipped through her fingers a long time ago. "We were happy in the beginning, though I suppose that's how it always goes. When we got married, it started out small. He wouldn't let me have contractors come to the house unless he was there. Like, not even a plumber to fix the toilet. If other men hugged me, it was a big fight. He grew more possessive over time, so much that I dropped out of college and isolated myself from my friends and my mom.

"My mom came by one day while he was at work and packed up my things. I was so scared to leave him.

He lived for me. Lived to control me. He was nervous without me. It sounds stupid now, but staying made sense to me at the time." She runs her tongue over her lower lip. "It was bad. Anyway, my mom got me out, and I filed for a divorce. When he was served with the divorce papers, he..." Tavita pauses and finishes off her drink in a long glug. "He killed himself that day."

I don't know what to say, so I simply sit there, stunned by all she's been through.

Now I know why she clings to that stiff upper lip and her casual humor.

Tavita pours herself another drink. "So when Máximo explained that flip of my genetics, I had no reason to question it. My husband didn't love me; he was obsessed with me. I've learned there's quite the distinction."

Tio Bruno runs his hand over his mouth. "So it's true. La Ciguapa really does exist, and she's you."

Tavita nods, her face vacillating from apologetic to owning who she is. I love that she's not cowing to those who have a problem with the way she was born. "I was explaining to Adelita while you were out on your walk that it's not something I do on purpose. My father explained that it's part of my genetics. I give off a scent or something when I'm into someone and want a relationship. Once I decide I want to be with a man, if they want me even a little bit, they're infected with my mojo. They won't leave. And eventually, I might suck out their will."

I finally find my words. "You're a widow," I state plainly.

Tavita snorts. "Technically, I guess, but I don't see myself that way. I got out of a really frightening relationship, only to have my father tell me that might be the only kind I'll ever have."

Sympathy swirls in me. "No, Tavita. Not even close. You choose what you do with your genetics. You have a say in your life."

She looks at me with pity, as if I'm five and told her that Santa Claus is very much real. "I don't, actually. I didn't speak to you for days, Bruno. I tried so hard not to fall for you. I don't want to suck out your will."

I want to snort at the notion that anyone could tame this bull of a man.

Then again, he was here when we came to the house. It's clear he wants her, wants to be with her.

But the mythical will-sucking angle is something to consider, for certain.

Tio Bruno stays silent, so Tavita turns to me. "Both of Máximo's daughters are Ciguapas, Adelita. I'd hoped that wasn't the case, but I'm certain you've had an effect on Santos and Cruz."

My mouth dries. "What do I do? I don't want to hurt them. I don't want to turn something good into a scary situation."

Tavita shrugs, which is the opposite of reassuring. "I have to be extra careful. Bruno has a strong will, and I don't go out of my way to tame him. I'm hoping if he knows I like him bullheaded, he won't try to change to be something different."

I mull over her logic. "I like that." I finish off my drink and reach for the bottle, refilling my glass because apparently, I'm a mythological creature come to life. Whiskey seems in order for such conversations.

Tio Bruno picks up his glass and drains it. "So I can leave if I want? You're not going to try to make me stay?"

Tavita covers over the hurt I catch flashing across her vision. "Door's only locked to outsiders. You can go any time you like. That's not new information. I just have to be careful not to lean on you too much, because you'll start to sacrifice the good parts of yourself to prop me up. I don't want that. I've seen where that leads, and how it ends."

I drink the second glass quicker than the first while the two of them go back and forth on the specifics of testing out their relationship, given this new information. They're so adult about it, not giving in to the urge to get possessive or overly anxious.

I guess Tio Bruno limits himself to one freak-out per night.

The food comes, but I'm not hungry. None of us are, but Tio Bruno sets the bag down on the counter and doles out the burritos. "Goat meat from my favorite spot. Eat." It's a command, not a request.

Now I doubly don't want to take a bite. I don't like being ordered around. My own mom never talked to me like that. She didn't have to.

Instead I drink, picking at the filling of my burrito while I sip on my third glass, relishing the way the room tilts and blurs my worries. I don't want to think about any of this. I don't want to be mired in things that can't get better.

The guys are in danger of having their wills sucked out by me. Judging by the way Santos let me talk him into getting his picture taken, it's already happening.

I hum to myself while Tio Bruno and Tavita keep on talking between bites. When she gets a spot of sauce on her lip, his thumb is quick to sweep it away. He pops his digit into her mouth, his eyes lidded while she sucks the red stickiness away.

Yeah, no matter how affronted Tio Bruno is that he's been had by Tavita's hypnotic genetics, there's no question that he will stay with her.

I should give them some time to themselves.

After I finish my drink.

The whiskey is strong, just how I like it when the world has too many details that can't be fixed. Tavita nudges my burrito closer to me, but I ignore it. I'm not hungry. I'm sick to my stomach, thinking of how I'm going to break this news to Cruz and Santos.

They'll leave, as they should. They didn't mean to fall for me.

When I reach for the bottle to pour myself another, the scattered shape of Tio Bruno stills my hand. "That's enough for you, lightweight. You're going to throw up all over the place if you don't slow down."

"They're going to leave," I state simply.

Tavita tuts me. "You don't know that. And there's nothing the whiskey can solve tonight. Bruno's right. Drink some water, honey-girl."

"Can I sleep on your couch?" I reach for the glass of water she hands me, but my aim is off, so she tips the cup to my lips, standing beside me. Her fingers comb through my damp hair as she rests my head to her side.

"Of course. You can sleep in my bed with me, if you like."

"No, the couch is good." Then I whisper up at her, "Tio Bruno wants to have sexy sex with you."

Tio Bruno chokes through a laugh, so I'm guessing

my whisper wasn't as quiet as I'd hoped. "I definitely don't want you in the room for that, half-pint."

I stick my tongue out at him, because when I'm on the road to drunk, I turn into the mouthy adolescent I never dared to be, back when those sorts of antics would have been age-appropriate.

I drink the water Tavita gives me until I can't take another sip. "The couch is that way?" I ask, pointing over my shoulder.

Tavita redirects my hand. "That way, actually. I'll help you."

"Nah. I got it. I'm the almighty See-glop-ah. I can trail the blaze to the couch without a guide." I stand, but regret my bravado immediately. The room spins, tilting violently on its side. Or maybe I'm the one who's spinning and falling. I can't tell.

Either way, I don't care that Cruz and Santos are going to end up as shells of the men they could have been before I got my hooks into them. I don't care at all. About anything.

My whole body levitates, because I'm just that magical.

Or maybe it's because Tio Bruno's face is near mine. Is he carrying me? Aw, the old softy. I mean to pat his rough cheek as he takes me to the couch, but my hand is too heavy to aim properly, so I end up smacking myself in the face by mistake.

He chuckles because he's an ass, which is exactly what I tell him.

"Is that so? If I was an ass, I suppose I could drop you on the floor right here. But I don't think your sister would want to have sexy sex with me if I did that."

"You hate Cruz," I mutter as he lays me across the brown couch.

Tio Bruno freezes, his hand still beneath my ribs as he remains bent over my form. "I do not. He's my nephew."

"He's your tool. When was the last time you hugged him?"

"You're drunk." Tio Bruno frowns at me, so I know he's still himself. If he was all gooey-eyed and grinning, then I'd know his brain had been stolen by the La-see-gloppy.

"I'm right. I never get to say that. Whenever my patients ignore me and their life blows up in their faces, you know what I never get to say? I'm right. It feels so good!" I grip onto his shirt to keep the world from spinning. "I'm right, and you'll lose him. You'll die alone because you never learned how to hug. You know what's sad about that?"

Tio Bruno stares at me looking truly hurt. "What?"

I lose my hold on his shirt. "Everything."

Tavita scoots into my vision, rolling me onto my side and covering me with a thick blanket. "Okay, champ. Next time, you're stopping at one drink. The trash can is right here, in case you need to puke in the night. I'm going to turn in."

Tio Bruno straightens. "Do you want me to come with you?"

Even through my haze, I can see his vulnerability clearly.

Tavita shrugs. "You know I want you, Beautiful. But it's your choice. I'm okay either way."

No, she's not. She wants him badly, I can tell. But she's unwilling to say anything that might silence his inner voice that tells him what he wants and what he doesn't.

Tio Bruno jabs a finger at me. "Don't be a problem."

Because I'm a jerk, I call after him, "Don't be bad in bed!"

He cringes, but follows after Tavita, closing the door behind them.

20

BREAKING AND ENTERING

CRUZ

Rafi tracked me down and brought me home, but when I got there, Adelita was gone. Santos talked me down as best he could, but I couldn't sleep until I checked myself to make sure she was at her sister's house. Of course, I forgot which place belongs to Tavita, so I picked three wrong locks before I found my sweet Addy passed out on the brown couch.

The furniture is so plain, and Adelita so stunning. It's wrong that she's sleeping on something so beneath her status. I'm tempted to pick her up and carry her back to the house, but something tells me that would be overstepping. Plus, it's still storming outside, thanks to me.

I creep into the living room, catching a banging rhythm coming from the back, along with what sounds like two whales groaning. My brows raise because, while I knew Tio Bruno had a thing for Tavita, I didn't realize they were actually sleeping together.

Loudly.

The moonlight shines through a sliver in the curtains, illuminating the face of my angel. She's so beautiful, so very perfect. I can't believe I attacked my own uncle today. But if it kept her from being further hurt, I can't bring myself to regret my actions. Not fully.

I kneel by her side, knowing I shouldn't be here. But I don't want to sleep without her. Not only is it terrifying and possibly dangerous, but even if La Sayona wasn't an issue, being near Adelita calms me down. I should learn how to do that without her, but I never saw much value in it until she came into the picture. Now I notice if I've been apart from her for too long. Everything in me tenses too much, refusing to loosen until she's with me.

I shouldn't touch her cheek, but I can't not. Her lips are parted in slumber, and I smell whiskey on her breath. Adelita doesn't drink, not that I'm aware of.

I scared her. I really scared her. I lost my temper and turned into a man who fights his own family. That shouldn't be me, but looking back, I know it is, and it would be again if I was in the same situation. I need her to be safe, to be okay.

Santos promised me that Tio Bruno was looking

after her, but obviously that's not happening. She's unguarded and drank herself to sleep.

Dang, her skin is soft.

When Adelita lets out a low moan, I worry I've been made. But she only reaches around until her hand falls on the trash bin. I move out of the way as she slips off the couch onto her knees, holding the trash can like it's a cuddly teddy bear. She sees me, but it doesn't look like it registers that I'm not supposed to be here.

So I stay. I gather her hair up into my fist with one hand and rub slow circles into her back with the other. "Easy, baby. It's alright."

"I'm going to be sick."

"I know. Get it all out and you'll feel much better. How much did you drink?"

"All of it," she admits. "I'm a See-gloppy."

I have no idea what she's talking about, and I doubt she does either. "You're *my* see-gloppy, got it? You want to crash somewhere, that's fine. But if you're going to drink yourself stupid, save some for me next time."

"It's not a myth." Then she burps over the trash can. "I don't feel so good."

"Can you make it to the bathroom?"

"I don't know."

"Let's give it a try. We'll take the trash can with us just in case."

I'm careful as I help her to her feet, supporting her elbow so she has someone to lean on while her world tilts and eventually makes her vomit. Even when I hear my uncle climax to the tune of a donkey's bray from the bedroom down the hall, I don't falter.

We make it to the bathroom just in time.

I've never been the nurturing type, but I don't mind holding her hair back while she barfs more than anyone I've ever seen. My fighting made my girlfriend sick, so whatever rights I thought I had to my temper, it's clear to me those aren't as important as this. Fat tears roll down her cheeks while her lower lip quivers between breaths.

The sight breaks my heart—an organ I never saw much use for, but now leads me around like a dog on a leash. I kneel beside her, yanking the towel off the bar and working it under her knees so she doesn't bruise them on the hard floor.

Adelita loses more than her lunch into the toilet. It's several dinners' worth. Coming off the heels of being starved by the Kalku, throwing up isn't what the doctor ordered.

I took off on her. I got scared and I ran. And now I'm holding her hair back while floods of stomach acid pour out of her, though gratefully, after a few minutes, that's coming less often. At least she can get in a few sobs between each bout of sick.

When she finally stops, she's as weak as a daisy. I help her to wash out her mouth and gargle with something minty, but that's all the standing she can do. Carrying her is an easy choice. I love doing it, except for the fact that I'm soaked and she's shivering. I lay her back down on the couch on her side, covering her with the fleece blanket.

She won't touch the water I offer her, merely moaning and closing her eyes. "Gross."

She's cute like this—unpolished and borderline grouchy.

I should go home, but that's as far as the debate goes. I stay right where I am, ganking the extra throw pillow off the end of the couch and tucking it under my cheek as I spread out on the floor beside the couch. If anyone tries to get at her, they'll have to go through me.

I don't care if I've lost my mind; I've never felt calmer than sleeping on the floor, knowing that if she needs me, I'll be right there.

21

DAYLIGHT CONFESSIONS
CRUZ

Tavita's cry of distress wakes me roughly, dragging my torso to sit up. "What's wrong?"

"You! Did you... Did you break in last night so you could sleep by her?" Tavita shakes her head at me, pulling a man's shirt down further to cover her bare legs.

Not any man's shirt. She's wearing my uncle's undershirt.

I raise my chin with indignance. "Santos promised me Tio Bruno would watch over her, but I was able to pick the locks no problem."

We're being too loud. Adelita groans and rolls onto her back. "No shouting. My head hurts."

Tavita shakes her head in worried astonishment. "You are insane, Mister. We're in the village. The only person breaking in to get at her is you!"

"And I found her unguarded!"

Tio Bruno comes out, shirtless and in his boxer briefs, scratching his hairy chest. "What's the problem?"

I grimace at the post-coital sight of the two of them, especially when Tavita leans against his chest contentedly. *Yuck.* "There's no problem. Now that you're up and ready to look after things, I'll go on home and wash up."

"Ho, no. We're talking about this right now." Tavita points to Adelita, who groans again and flails, losing her fight with the blanket.

I peel the fabric down to free her. "Easy, baby. Let's get some water in you."

"Cruz?" she mumbles, her eyes mostly closed. Her lips are puffy from sleep, but I restrain myself from kissing her until she's awake enough to actually consent. "When did you get here?"

I can't help my chuckle. "Water," I insist. "Water and something greasy."

Tio Bruno rummages in the fridge, coming back with a cold burrito. "This should do it. If you can keep this down, you're golden."

Adelita gags at the smell of the goat meat I know Tio Bruno loves. Still she takes a bite, washing it down with water that makes her moan with discomfort.

I sit on the couch beside her, my arm around her shoulders to keep her upright.

Tavita comes back into the room with sweatpants on, thank goodness, and my uncle does the same. It's weird to see them so casual with each other, but I suppose I get similar looks from people whenever I make my affections for Adelita known.

Tavita leans against the wall, but Tio Bruno won't have it. He drags in a stool from the kitchen and helps her sit on it, his hand on her back.

Bizarre.

"Cruz, I have to tell you a few things." Then Tavita pauses and gets up, yanking the front door open and peeking her head out. "I see you, Santos. In you get." Then she mumbles as she resumes her spot on the stool, "If that isn't proof, I don't know what is."

Santos comes in as a wolf, trotting across the wooden floor and sitting at Adelita's feet. He sniffs her toes and her shin, whining until her hand tangles in his fur.

"Incorrigible," Tavita scolds, though she doesn't seem terribly surprised. "Boys, listen up. There are things you need to know about Adelita and myself."

Then Tavita proceeds to break down things I never knew could be true. Sure, I've heard of La Ciguapa, but it's a myth. Everyone knows that. Yet as Tavita points out aspects of our relationship, down to the fact that neither of us could spend the night without her, dread begins to churn in my gut. I don't know if I'm worried that I'll be the fated man who gets his will sucked dry, leaving me as a husk of abuse and worry, like Tavita's deceased husband, or if I'm frightened I can feel Adelita withdrawing as her genetic cards are laid out on the table.

"I don't want to control you two!" Adelita frets, hugging the garbage can on her lap. "I didn't know! You have to believe me. I would never do anything to hurt either of you."

Santos can't tolerate the torment in her tone any more than I can. He transforms, taking the spot on her other side on the couch. He's wet, but he doesn't hesitate to wrap his arms around her. "I know that. I knew from the beginning what you were. That doesn't scare me. Those legends focus on the men who succumb to being lesser versions of themselves. Being with you gave me my voice back. I'm not scared of you, Adelita, though I can tell you're frightened of yourself."

"How can you say that? What if I turn you into Tavita's husband? What if you get so obsessed with our relationship that you keep me away from other people?"

At this, Santos and I share a much-needed laugh. Santos smiles at her. "Oh, good. I thought you were seriously upset. Thanks for making a joke."

She balks at us. "I'm being totally serious."

Santos' face sours. "I'm currently dating you and

Cruz. If I was going to get possessive, I think it would have happened back then when you first started having feelings for him."

I roll my eyes. "I'm not dating you, Santos. We're both dating Adelita."

Santos' mouth pulls to the side as he examines his words. "I see no difference."

Tavita points to the three of us. "But see? Adelita made it clear that she wanted the both of you, and suddenly, you two wanted the same thing. It's the power of La Ciguapa. Whatever she wants, you're not going to deny her. If my sister was anyone else, you two would be in serious trouble, but she's not greedy or manipulative, so who knows? It might actually work out between the three of you. Crazier things have happened."

Tavita's words of caution are white noise. "Look, I know Adelita well enough to understand that I want to be with her. If she comes with Santos, fine by me. But I'm not about to spend my nights away from her."

Santos' neck shrinks. "I tried. Really, I did. I made it all the way back to the house. But I didn't last long. I respected your wishes and gave you your space, though. I slept out in the woods so I could watch the house."

Adelita narrows an eye at him, but that's the most she'll disapprove. Still, Santos has the grace to look mildly abashed.

Santos runs his hand over hers. "I knew what you were from the beginning. I know the Kalku have some strange beliefs, but La Ciguapa was never a myth to me. I chose you before you ever turned your affections my way, Adelita. And judging by how long it took you and Cruz to get together, I'm guessing it was the same for the two of you. The evil stories of La Ciguapa center around a woman who goes around purposefully luring men in, making them fall in love with her for sport. That's not what happened." His gaze connects with mine. "Adelita's love never turns sour like that because she's not selfish."

I finish the thought. "And we're not psychopaths. I don't want to control her."

"Help is the sunlit side of control," Tavita says sagely. "You broke into my house last night to *help* her."

I don't need this crap. "Yes, I broke into your house and didn't drag Addy back to mine. I stayed with her while she was up sick. There's a difference."

Adelita groans. "That wasn't a dream? Oh, no. Cruz, gross. I didn't want you to see me like that!"

Tio Bruno dumps coffee grounds into the machine on the kitchen counter and turns it on. "Then don't drink so much next time. And eat as much of that burrito as you can. Finish the thing off, half-pint." Then to Tavita he says, "How do you like your coffee, Blue Eyes?"

Tavita softens at the nickname. "I want my coffee to taste like a cavity. The sweeter the better, Beautiful. There's a hot cocoa canister just there. Two scoops."

Tio Bruno blanches in time with me, but neither of us says anything. We take our coffee black. Anything else is a bastardization.

It's so oddly normal, this morning routine. It's weird to watch Tio Bruno be so human, making coffee and not criticizing her for liking something disgusting and childish.

I guess he really is smitten by La Ciguapa.

Holy fates, so am I.

When Adelita leans her head against Santos' cheek, he turns her body so he can hold her in his arms. Without thinking, I reach down and lift her legs, stretching them across my lap so I can warm her toes, massaging them lightly. When I see her lids drooping, I arrest her burrito from her feeble fingertips and set it on the end table. Within seconds, Adelita is fast asleep in Santos' arms, making him the happiest man on earth. He loves it when she trusts him. He lives to meet the few needs she expresses.

I know the feeling.

Yikes. Maybe I do need to slow things down. Yet, when I contemplate removing her legs from my lap, my gut hollows. I like the weight of her on me.

"You're in it now," Tavita says quietly. "Careful, boys. Take it slow. The slower the better."

But as Tavita walks into the kitchen to show Tio Bruno how she likes her coffee, my gaze drifts to Adelita's sleeping face. I mentally move the rest of her things and Santos' into my bedroom, knowing that neither of us will stomach being parted from her ever again.

22

THICK SKULL
ADELITA

I haven't laughed this hard in ages. Watching Cruz and Santos try to paint sugar skulls while the children in the village mock their simplistic designs is fantastic. Cruz's fingers are too thick; he's broken three sugar skulls so far, making me laugh harder each time. Unsurprisingly, Santos is careful with his, but he doesn't branch out to more than the one pot of color that's closest to him.

"You're supposed to make it cool," one of the kids chides them both. "Like with lots of colors and designs. See mine? The eyes are fireworks."

Cruz grumbles and Santos' mouth draws to the side as he eyes the different hues out of reach. He's too humble to ask for what he wants, so when his gaze catches on the teal pot, I push it toward him.

"This was a bad idea," Cruz tells me yet again. "Painting with a bunch of kids? I don't see why anyone would want to spend their day like this."

"You don't have to," I point out, finishing the purple flower on the cheek of my skull. "I want to get to know the people here, and Eva suggested the community center. This was the event listed for the day, so I signed up. I didn't sign you up. You did that all on your own."

"I'm regretting that choice every second."

"This is good for me. We're out protecting a village I've never explored. I want to be part of your hometown, Cruz. This is my way of doing that."

A smile threatens to shatter his grumping. "I guess I can appreciate that."

I kiss Cruz's cheek, grinning like an idiot. I haven't painted in years. I'm no good at it, but I've learned you don't have to be amazing at something to enjoy doing it. I point at the little girl's sugar skull who's sitting across from me. "How'd you do the stem like that? It's so curvy."

The child lights up and practically lunges over the table to give me a close-up demonstration. She's adorable. She's missing three teeth and her hair is worn in two long braids. I love the rascally look about her. There's a point to her nose that makes me want to pinch it, but as I don't actually know her, I refrain. I catch her name scrawled on the side, marking her artistry.

"That's really cool, Leticia."

Leticia frowns at Santos. "You don't want teal for flowers. Try pink. Pink is best." She takes the brush from his fingers because, when you're eight, you can do things like that.

Unless you have a mother who disapproves. "No! Leticia, stay back. Don't touch him." She jerks her daughter backward to plop her on the bench opposite us. The wariness in the mother's eyes is directed at Santos, as if he'd committed the faux-pas, and not Leticia.

It's not the first time I've caught sight of the parents guarding their children from Santos. I've largely ignored the circumspect scowls, telling myself that they just haven't had time to get used to Santos being out and about in the village. The guys are always traveling, after all.

Rafi doesn't like their wary stares and whispers, either. "Funny thing about Santos. He likes beautiful things. Teal flowers, nature scenes. How about you, Leticia? Do you like flowers?"

Leticia talks with her hands. "Love them. I planted some with Mommy last week. They haven't sprouted up yet." Her nose crinkles. "How long does it take?"

"A hundred years," Rafi complains, not holding back his natural propensity for theatrics. He glances across the table. "Santos, which kind of flower is your favorite?"

Santos shrugs. "I didn't grow up around many flowers. The plant I found most useful was aloe. Healed burns, helped with ulcers when I boiled the spines in a pot of water, and did other useful things like that. So I think aloe is my favorite."

Rafi points to Santos with his brush. "Santos likes things that heal people. I think that's nice."

I'm struck with the beauty in the simple truth. I love that even though Santos was raised by horrific men, his true goodness wasn't crushed.

Leticia grins, showing off the gap in her mouth. "So nice. I like anything yellow. Yellow is happy."

Rafi chuckles. "I suppose it is. Santos, which plants have yellow in them?"

Santos rattles off a list of plants, some of which I've never heard of. Leticia is enraptured, leaning closer and interjecting questions every now and then. "What's that one you just said?"

"Goldenrod?" Santos replies. "It helps reduce inflammation and can calm muscle spasms."

Leticia looks crestfallen. "Oh. I was hoping it grew gold or something."

Santos' eyebrows bunch. "What do you need gold for?"

"To buy things."

"What kinds of things?"

"Candy. A new bike. A frog."

His lips purse. "You want gold so you can buy a frog?" Santos with a little girl is just about the cutest thing. He turns and pecks my cheek. "I'll be back. You got Adelita, Cruz?"

Cruz's arm loops around my hips. "Of course."

They're so funny about my safety. I get why, but still. We're at a children's community center event. It's not exactly rife with danger.

Rafi paints, but his happiness level has fallen at not being able to draw Santos in. It's our first day out and about in the community, enjoying Cáceres for more than a brisk walk. I didn't expect things to be perfect. Santos sees himself as an outsider. Until that changes, no one else will see him as a citizen who belongs.

No matter. I'm an outsider, too. We'll figure it out.

"It's not going to work," Tio Bruno chides from the other end of the table.

I bristle at the insinuation that anything I try might not have a one hundred percent success rate. "Paint your skull, old man."

Tio Bruno hasn't touched his sugar skull, but at least

Tavita got him to sit at the table. All the parents are standing around chatting, some knitting or juggling babies. We're the only adults at the long rectangular tables that stretch end to end across the community center. The construction paper doodles on the wall clash terribly with Tio Bruno's scowl.

"Everyone here is afraid of what they don't understand, and no one but the three of you understands Santos. Pace yourself. It's a long road to where you want to get to."

Tavita's brushstrokes on her skull are dainty and calculated. "Something tells me you all have forgotten the point of today. Adelita and I are getting to know your village because this is our home now. If you want us to stick around here, then don't be annoying." Then she paints a streak of purple down the slope of Tio Bruno's nose, which, I'll admit, takes my mind off of things quite nicely.

Tio Bruno frowns at her, but he doesn't wipe off the paint. A few of the parents surrounding the tables cover their mouths to hide their surprise. The foreboding military commander never does anything goofy, yet there he sits, letting Tavita paint him up for her amusement.

I love it. I love them together. But the second she

frowns in his direction, I'll be the first one to shove him out the door.

Cruz grits his teeth as he tries to be careful with his skull, but the cheekbone cracks off. He bites back a cuss word, remembering that we are surrounded by children. Roberto slides Cruz's mess toward himself and glues the busted part back on with the edible white paste. "There," he tells his big brother in a conspiratorial whisper. "Now no one will know."

Eva saunters into the community center, mouth agape. "Am I hallucinating?" She pulls out her phone, taking pictures of everyone at the table. "Dad's not going to believe this. I need photographic evidence. Are you actually painting?"

Cruz glares at his sister. "One more word, and I'm leaving."

Eva switches her focus to her surly uncle. "I don't understand. Are you making him do this as some sort of punishment?"

Tio Bruno shakes his head. "Tavita suggested I take a break at lunch and come here so she could acquaint herself with the villagers. Adelita and the guys are doing the same."

"You're taking a lunch break? Like, for fun?" She glances around. "I don't get it. What's your angle?" She plops down beside Roberto, addressing Cruz after kissing the top of Roberto's head. "And you're still here. It's been a week since you came back. You're never home for a whole week. What gives?"

"Sick of me already?" Cruz teases. When Eva stares him down, he cracks. "The guys and I are slowing down. Tio Bruno's already sent a group out to take what would have been our next assignment." When Eva appears shocked and still needing information, he adds, "I'm tired of always being on the road. Thought I'd help out here instead."

Rafael grins at Eva. "It's not supposed to make sense, Sis. The simpler explanation is that we've all had lobotomies, which have changed our minds about constant travel."

Eva chuckles at him. "That, I could believe."

Cruz shoves his sugar skull away from him in frustration. "I can't do this! Mine is rigged. It keeps breaking."

I stifle my giggle while Roberto starts working with the paste on Cruz's mess. The chin crumbled off, and Cruz is pouting like a baby about it.

Tio Bruno hands Tavita a pot of paint that's just out of reach. "Figured I'd spend the day with Tavita before I head out for the island."

Eva nods. "Ah. Okay. Now this whole scene makes a

little more sense. She's punishing you with fun for leaving her here."

Tavita and Eva don't know each other all that well yet, but Tavita isn't one for holding back. "Actually, I'm going with Bruno to the island. So is Rafi. Cruz and Santos are staying behind with Adelita."

My hand freezes. "What? I thought I was going. I've been training every day for a week!"

Tio Bruno's cool demeanor makes me livid. "Yes, and you fight like a person who's had one whole week of training. You're not ready. You go over there, you die. Santos and Cruz weren't willing to leave you unprotected, so they're staying behind. That's the compromise."

"That's not the compromise I asked for! I wanted to go with you. Come on, Tio Bruno. You know I'd be an asset." Because others are within earshot, I don't mention my super strength aloud.

Tio Bruno is unperturbed with my frustration. "You say asset, I say liability. Máximo wants you on the island, half-pint. So no way are you going over there. Not on my watch."

I point in accusation at my sister. "How come Tavi gets to go?"

Tavita bats her lashes in my direction. "I asked really, really nicely."

I blanch at the insinuation. It weirds me out every time I'm forced to see Tio Bruno as a human with romantic tendencies instead of the donkey he's always been in my eyes.

"I have to go," Tio Bruno explains. "Cruz and Santos don't. Tavita knows the lay of the island, so she's an asset." He fiddles with a paintbrush. "She can find the Luz Mala."

"You suck," I tell Tio Bruno, who smirks at me with pride at having thoroughly pissed me off.

I finish painting my skull, and though I'm proud of myself for making something and taking time to paint for fun, it looks worse than any of the children's creations at the table. I decide I'm okay with that.

Cruz does not take to defeat easily. By the time he calls it quits, his sugar skull is the domed top of the head and nothing else. Roberto takes the crumbled pieces and glues them onto his own creation, making a monster that produces growling noises as he walks it along the table top.

"You're upset," Cruz points out, massaging my nape.

"I'm holding you back," I say quietly. "Of course I'm upset. You love going on missions. You hate family stuff and fun. You're already letting me suck out your will."

He laces his fingers through mine under the table. "Let's go for a walk."

I hand Eva my sugar skull. "See if you can make it... not look like this." The whole thing was supposed to be flowers, but it just looks like a series of splotches.

Eva gets to work, because making things beautiful is easy for her.

I can only hope I will be able to add just as notable a contribution to Cáceres someday.

23

SCARY YELLOW FLOWERS
ADELITA

I go where Cruz leads, exiting the community center and making our way toward the back of the building, away from prying eyes. No matter where we go, people stare. No one has ever seen Cruz with a woman, or Santos, for that matter.

"See that?" Cruz says, squeezing my hand. "I wanted to go for a walk and I asked for what I wanted, even though you were happy to stay there and strike up a fight with Tio Bruno. You're not sucking out my will. That's never been you. And giving up what I want? That's never been me. This is going to work, Addy. You just have to trust it a little bit. This whole La Ciguapa thing is messing with our heads. We can't let it take over."

I lean against the wooden wall of the building,

resting the back of my head there as I close my eyes. "But it's already happening. You love traveling. You hate being in the village. You're going to resent me for keeping you in place. That's not what I'm trying to do. Tío Bruno can train me when he gets back. I'll be ready for the road soon enough. You don't have to give up the life you love to be with me."

Cruz stands before me, his head tilted to the side with a smirk, like he thinks I'm trying to be cute. "Did it ever occur to you that I was running from Cáceres, and now I don't want to? Every time I cried out in the night, it triggered my dad, who never wanted the curse passed down to me. He remembers the torture he had to endure for years. I wanted to take the curse away from him, so he could have a normal life with Consuela and the kids. And I didn't want people to look at me with pity in their eyes, thinking of La Sayona. Now that she's gone, I don't feel so much like running anymore. I can stay in place for once."

I stare at our joined fingers. "I didn't think of it like that. You love your dad, making yourself suffer outside the home so your dad doesn't have to hear how painful it all is for you. That's very sweet."

"Life in Cáceres was hard for Santos, too. I don't want Santos subjected to their fears of him. It's hard to watch them ostracize him. Even painting a sugar skull, the parents don't want him near their kids. He doesn't deserve that."

"No, he doesn't."

"Now that La Sayona doesn't have me so on edge, I want to take some time to get him acclimated to the village for real. Not just get them to tolerate his presence, but do more things like this—the painting, hanging out in public places in Cáceres. Stuff where he's in their faces, at their tables." Cruz tugs me toward him, wrapping our joined hands behind me so he can tuck his thumb into the waist of my jeans at the small of my back. "Don't for one second think I don't want to be here with you. I don't want to spend all our time separated by seatbelts." His voice turns serious as he looks around to confirm we're alone. "One day, I'm going to be the chief of Cáceres. I think it's time I stop running away from the people I've been protecting."

I reach up with my free hand and stroke my fingers across his broad chest. I love the firm feel of his intimidating musculature. "You're going to be a great leader."

"I'm going to be tolerated," he corrects glumly, "unless I put in some face time with them. Figure out what makes them tick, fix the daily frustrations that keep people from uniting."

"They're not united?"

"It's human nature to focus on the things that we

hate or what's different instead of celebrating what makes us come together. For instance, did you notice a few of the parents pointing at a leak in the roof of the community center?"

"I didn't," I admit. "Is that something you know how to fix?"

"No, but they do. And they can teach me how, rather than complaining about it." He brushes his nose across mine. "And the border wall. I think it's doing more harm than good."

Hope rises in my chest. "You do?"

"It's clear that we haven't been helping refugees as we should. We pat ourselves on the back when we go in and rescue them, but we have no plan for getting people on their feet, outside of slapping on some band-aids and sending them back out into the world. That's not right." His thumb touches on my skin under my shirt. "If you hadn't come into the picture, I don't think I would have truly understood how little our rescues actually help if we drop the ball like we've been doing. We need to let refugees stay here. Their homes weren't good enough protection to keep them safe; they should have the option of staying in Cáceres. Otherwise, what did we do all this for?"

Pure love rises up in me and splashes all over this great leader. I lift up on my toes and kiss Cruz without warning. Well, the warning that a kiss was coming should have been when he spoke altruistically, but Cruz makes a noise of surprise when my lips touch on his, as if he doesn't understand that unselfishness is a turn on.

His facial hair always adds a brush of prickle to contrast the softness of his lips. He tastes like warmth and something sweet. Has he been sneaking bites of his sugar skull?

Cruz backs me up until my butt hits the wall, deepening the kiss because that's exactly what we want to do. In all the mess of Máximo, myths and mayhem, it's the stolen moments like this that remind me what it's all for.

"I'm going to stay here," Cruz tells me between kisses, "and my dad is going to show me more about a chief's duties." His tongue pillages my mouth, stealing a gasp from me. He usually takes our kisses so slowly, but this one picks up. He sucks hard on my lower lip, letting loose little noises of pleasure that make me feel treasured, and like I actually might belong exactly here. "More," he begs, kissing harder.

I gnaw on his lip, meeting his aggression with a little of my own. This is our time in the daylight, sneaking around the building like a couple of teenagers. When I scrape across his nipple through his shirt, Cruz jerks against me. The passion hits a new height as he presses his hips to mine with a guttural growl.

It's all I can do to remind myself I cannot strip his shirt off and trace his muscles with my tongue. Cruz grips my hip, pushing his thumb into the dip so he can play in the space between the material and my bare skin.

I love kissing this man. Even when he pulls away, his chin jerking to the side with a frown, I'm enamored of his profile.

"No!" A woman cries from inside.

Cruz and I spring into action, bolting from the spot. We rush back inside the building, ready to defend our little artists.

Only there's nothing amiss that I can tell. Santos came back, but he's clear across the room, his hands up in surrender while Leticia's mother rips her daughter off the bench. "Don't come near my daughter ever again!"

"Whoa. What happened?" Cruz beelines toward Santos, checking his face and hands. "Are you alright?"

Tio Bruno is on his feet, but his face is shrouded with that unreadable frown he always wears. "Santos gave the child a box."

I glance at the abandoned shipping box on the table, examining the mother's fear and Leticia's angst. "He came near my daughter," she explains, her lips tight as she pushes Leticia behind her. "He shouldn't be here.

This is where we bring our children. The cave slave doesn't belong near us. He is not from Cáceres!"

It's like her words have grown a hand and slapped me across the face. I should let Cruz handle this, but I cannot keep quiet at the injustice. "Why would you say that? Santos' home address is in Cáceres. He is Don José's son. Santos has spent the last two years fighting the Kalku to keep the tribe safe. Doesn't that qualify him as a citizen? If not, then what does?"

"I was born here," she retorts, as if that makes any difference.

"I wasn't," I counter, challenging her to come up with a different asinine reason, "yet I respect Don José's judgment, adopting Santos into his home and making him a legal citizen here."

"If you were not born in Cáceres, then you don't belong here, either! If not for Cruz, neither of you would pollute Cáceres. We were supposed to be protected against you! Did you not see the border walls?"

Eva's upper lip curls. "You would rather our bloodline die out than see Cruz marry someone outside of Cáceres? Your disrespect to my father has been noted."

Why do people always jump to Cruz and me getting married? I mean, honestly.

The woman guffaws, pointing at Santos. "His teeth are sharpened! He could tear out my little girl's throat!"

My nose crinkles as I rear back. "What?"

Eva stands, making her way to me. "Let it go, Adelita. They will never accept him. It's just the way it is."

My nostrils flair in rebellion. "Not while I'm here, it's not. Don José trusts Santos enough to live under his roof. Do you think the chief is an idiot? Because if you do, I want to hear it. That sort of talk is definitely not welcome when I'm around."

The woman pales. "Of course not."

"Santos has lived here for two years. Has he torn out any throats the entire time he's been here?"

"None that I know of, but..."

I posture, having hit my limit the second Santos appeared distressed. "Tio Bruno, is Santos an asset to the tribe? Is he a soldier you rely on and trust?"

Tio Bruno nods. "Without question. Our village is safer than any of the others. Cáceres hasn't seen a breach of the Kalku in the village since Santos got here. He's helped us understand their methods so we can protect ourselves against them."

Tavita eyes me with a glimmer of pride, but I'm too worked up to relish the feel of her approval. I march over to the table and peek into the box that's sparked so much controversy. My heart melts off a chunk of my rage as I shut the lid, noting the holes Santos poked in the top. "Santos, this is precious. You caught her a frog?"

Santos is trembling, but he manages a nod. "She said she wanted gold so she could buy a frog. She should save her gold. I can catch her a frog for free."

"And yellow flowers in here for her, too. Because she likes yellow flowers best. This is sweet." I turn my chin over my shoulder as Leticia twists out of her mother's reach and dashes for the box. "Well done. You saved your daughter from kindness."

Leticia squeals with delight, peering under the corner of the lifted lid so she can spy on her present. "Oh, thank you! I love him! Santos, what's his name?"

Santos looks like he very much wants to vanish from sight. "Whatever you like. I'm sorry!" He holds Cruz's gaze. "Can I go now? Can this be over?"

Cruz pauses but then finally nods. "Sure, Brother." Then he hugs Santos and kisses his cheek. When Cruz pulls back, he casts Rafi a resigned look. "It was a good try, spending some time in the village."

Rafi moves to Santos' side. "I'll go back to the house with you. Come on."

Santos can't get out of here quick enough. It's a heartbreaking sight to watch him race to the exit, giving everyone outside our little group a wide berth so they don't think he's dangerous. But it dawns on me that some of them always will. They will look at his smile and only see the monster they fear, rather than the man who brings them presents and keeps them safe.

Cruz folds me into his arms, scowling at the others for not coming to Santos' defense.

Then Cruz leans his fist on the table, aiming his attention at Leticia. "This frog's name is whatever makes you happy. Santos gave you that so you'd have an extra smile. Don't forget to show it off."

"Yes, Don Cruz!" She squeals again. "Diego Alejandro," she announces to the room, either oblivious to the lingering tension or too overjoyed to care. "He's my baby."

Cruz's nose crinkles. "Diego Alejandro? For a frog?"

She frowns up at him. "You said I could name him whatever I want."

Cruz rubs the nape of his neck. "I guess I did. Why Diego Alejandro?"

When she shrugs, I chime in with, "Because it's awesome. Roberto, what do you think?"

Roberto grins at the attention. "I think Diego Alejandro should have a slide in there. I can make one out of paper!"

And just like that, the kids lead the way in emotional intelligence, while the parents linger in the background, biting their nails that they cannot control the way the world turns.

24

THE RIGHT THING FOR CÁCERES
CRUZ

The morning always comes too quickly now. Before Adelita, if I woke before the sun, I counted it a blessing because La Sayona had less time to torture me. Now that I can sleep peacefully, when my alarm rings at eight in the morning, I debate shutting it off and going back to the good dream I was having.

Adelita groans beside me, and then stretches through a yawn. She does that most mornings, giving me an open invitation to coil my arm around her waist under the covers and nip at her breast through the silk of her nightgown. Her fingers twine through my hair, massaging and tugging, rousing me better than any alarm clock ever could.

Santos rolls onto his side and kisses the back of her

shoulder, his eyes still shut as he hooks a finger under her strap.

I love our mornings. If this was what all the guys grinned like idiots about when they found their woman, then count me chief of all idiots. Adelita's skin is soft and untested, yet she doesn't mind that I'm rough and unpolished. I started shaving with a better razor every morning, so I don't leave a sandpaper feel on her body. Little things are starting to matter to me more. I noticed the way she scoped my butt when I wore a certain pair of boxer briefs, so I bought more colors in that same style just to draw her eye. Got a haircut yesterday and made sure they trimmed down my sideburns.

I even told Eva to go nuts and redo my wardrobe, as well as Rafi's and Santos'. If we're going to be living in Cáceres full-time, might as well not look like I'm constantly on the road.

When Adelita climbs out of the bed to make her way to the bathroom, Santos sits up, finally fully awake. His voice is quiet as he confides in me. "Everyone leaves today. Half the army. Rafi. It feels wrong not to be with them. Santiago is my brother."

I can't imagine the conundrum Santos is mired in. He wants to go to the island to save his brother from Máximo, but his official job, as well as mine, is to protect Adelita. Both daughters of Máximo have been assigned two guards to make sure Máximo doesn't get his hands on them. When Tio Bruno ruled that Adelita wasn't ready to go to the island, he effectively benched Santos and me, too. We're not used to staying behind while other people do the fighting.

Santos draws his knees to his chest atop the mattress. "They leave in an hour, drive to the harbor, fight their way through the Kalku there, then sail to the island. If they meet the Massacooramaan, enough of the ships will get through, hopefully, to set foot on the island."

Santos has gone over the plan too many times to count, but I know saying the whole thing aloud helps him cope. If the army was going off on a half-cocked plan, that would amp up his worry. But the path is as solid as anyone can make it.

"When they get over to the island, Tavita will lead them to Máximo, where they'll..."

I finish his thought, because he gets stuck here every time. "Where they'll take Máximo down and free the captives, including Santiago. Then Rafi will bring our brother home to Cáceres. Simple as that."

Only we both know none of this will be simple. There's a reason no tribe has attempted a takedown of Máximo before. Máximo has access to magic we do not understand. He can take myth and make it reality—as evidenced by his daughters both being La Ciguapas. There is no end to his mystery and his might.

Half an army should be enough.

If it's not, we just lost half our tribe's defense.

I scrub my hands over my face. "We need to see to increasing security. The soldiers who are left behind need to be put to work, starting today. If Tio Bruno's job is getting to Máximo, then my job is to make sure the refugees have a safe place to escape to. It won't just be Santiago they're bringing to Cáceres."

That was me putting my foot down. Any rescues from the island are to be granted citizenship, should they want it. Cáceres is done rescuing people just to abandon them to happenstance.

Adelita couldn't keep her hands off me after that.

A knock on my door interrupts the lusty replay that races through my body.

"Come in."

Eva's eyes are rimmed in red, but she keeps her chin up, as if daring anyone to mention the fact that she's obviously been crying this morning. "Tio Bruno wants you at the barracks before he leaves. I'll be sitting in on a few council meetings today, seeing if I can help from that angle."

She's better at the chiefly duties than I am. I don't

understand how she can sit in meetings for hours at a time. I cannot stand talking when I could be doing.

"What's your plan?"

Eva opens my closet and starts pulling clothes out, spreading them on my bed. "We'll have fewer soldiers at our disposal and we're guarding a weapon Máximo needs."

I don't like Adelita being depersonalized, but I understand Eva's point. Adelita is a valuable weapon. Whatever Máximo wants, he cannot be allowed near.

"So, I'm going to suggest we ask the Mendez tribe for help guarding our outside borders, while our remaining troops keep watch inside the village."

I lean forward, thinking through Eva's plan. "I like that. You really think the Mendez people will go with it?"

"They owe us. They turned over Tavita to us because they were afraid to house her. They were afraid of Máximo's wrath. We're doing the heavy lifting, going after Máximo. It will benefit every tribe if this works." She searches through Santos' portion of the closet, keeping her eyes from us. "I've been thinking of reaching out to the Anzaldúa people, too."

I scoff. "They won't help. They're an underground society. They don't care who dies aboveground. They shut themselves off from us years ago."

Eva shrugs. "Even so, I'm extending the request. I'm not going to assume that just because they abandoned us before that they want to continue burying their heads in the sand. I don't want the tribes to be this divided. It's inefficient. We won't be able to take down Máximo without their help. It's all hands on deck."

I purse my lips. "Even if they lend us soldiers, it's not enough. It's a good start, but our people are still under fire as long as we house the daughters of Máximo." I massage a sore spot on my shoulder while I puzzle aloud. "Máximo knows Adelita is here. Maybe the thing we should ask Anzaldúa is if we can move her to their village. The signs will all point to Adelita being here, and we'll borrow extra soldiers from the Mendez tribe to protect our city, but Adelita will be in the one place no one would expect—Anzaldúa. The Kalku will attack here, but we'll have more than enough soldiers to fend them off, if the Mendez people help. The Kalku will exhaust their efforts getting into Cáceres, but Adelita will be in Anzaldúa."

Eva stills, her hand on one of my shirts. "I love it. Yes. I would suggest you and Santos stash her in a hotel somewhere remote, but putting her in Anzaldúa is even better. There's actual protection for her there. Plus, no one would suspect Anzaldúa and Cáceres would work together on anything."

My lips purse as we come to the inevitable road-block. "The only problem will be convincing Anzaldúa to hide Adelita."

In true little sister fashion, she waves off my valid concern. "Leave that to me. I'm very convincing."

I shake my head. "Every attempt Dad has made at establishing an ally relationship with their chief has been met with silence."

Eva shakes her head at my doubt. "I'll handle it."

Santos speaks up from the periphery. "The Anzaldúa people have no real army. They have a collection of farmers who rally when they need to, but as far as threats, they're nowhere near Máximo's radar. If we're borrowing troops from Mendez for our village, Máximo could deduce we'd hide her with them, since we're partnering with Mendez for protection. But we've never had a need to team up with the Anzaldúa people. They're not particularly useful to us or to Máximo. If we really wanted to hide Adelita, that's the best place."

I mull over the logic. The urge to backpedal is strong. "But there's no army in Anzaldúa."

Santos shrugs. "We wouldn't need one. The Kalku would never think to look for her there."

I shake my head, reminding them of the roadblock. "We have no political affiliations with Anzaldúa, though. I'm not sure they'd be willing to help us.

They've made it clear from the beginning that we're on our own."

Santos stands. "What better way to build trust between the villages than to team up to fight Máximo?"

Eva lays out an outfit for Santos. "And for the record, our giant border walls have made it clear from the moment they went up that Cáceres is only in it for ourselves. We're just as much to blame for not having Anzaldúa as an ally as they are." Then Eva moves to the door, but pauses and points to the clothes on our bed. "If I see either one of you in jeans and a black t-shirt, I'll use your bodies for fish bait to lure the Massacoora-maan away from Tio Bruno. Understood?"

I snigger, but stand before she fully exits. "Wait. Eva, are you really going to contact Anzaldúa?"

She nods, her jaw tight with resolve. "What makes you think I haven't done so already?"

I scoff my disbelief. "What? They don't communicate with anyone. They're an underground society."

Eva lifts her chin. "I've been corresponding with Salvador Gael for a few months, now."

"The prince of Anzaldúa? Are you serious? For what possible purpose?"

She sidesteps my inquiry. "I've been talking to Salvador long enough that I believe I can ask him for this favor." She smooths out a wrinkle on her long dress and then motions toward the bathroom, where Adelita is showering. "Adelita is my sister. My people are about to be targeted the second Tio Bruno leaves with half his army. I'll make whatever alliances I have to if it'll save Cáceres and our family."

It was me who worried about change, but Eva is unafraid to forge a better future for us all.

It is not the first time I've fostered unfettered respect for my sister, but this time, I can't help the words that come out of my mouth. "You should be chief, not me. You should lead Cáceres when Dad hands down the ruling spot. I never would have thought of any of this."

It's the only thing that stills my sister's exit. Her eyes climb slowly to me, and I can tell she's choosing her words carefully. "But you're firstborn. Tradition dictates the tribe will go to you."

I stand, crossing my arms over my chest. "But you know that's the wrong call. You're built for strategy on the political level. I'm not. I'm built for the battle field. The barracks suit me far better than the conference room. You making a plan to save our village in ways I never thought of? That suits you. If Cáceres answers to you?" I let the possibility unfold in the air for a few seconds before I pin a label on it. "Eva, there's no problem our tribe could not overcome."

Santos is frozen in place, but I can tell he doesn't think this is a bad idea.

Tears glisten in my sister's eyes as her lower lip quivers. "You would give up the ruling spot like that? Cruz, I don't think you know what you're saying. There's never been a woman leader in any tribe ever. The fact that you would even suggest that means so much to me. Thank you. Even though it could never happen, thank you."

I take a step toward her. "I don't care how it's always been done. This is how it should go. I care enough about Cáceres to do the right thing for her, even if it's never been tried." I motion between us.

A demure sob bursts out of Eva. I should know better than to tell her things like this, even if they're true. She dashes across the room and throws herself into my arms. "I love you, big brother. Even if it can't happen, I love that you want it to play out that way. I'll follow your lead on this. It's your call. I support you either way."

"I'll talk to Dad today. This is the right thing to do." I cup the back of her head, squeezing once before I release her. "You're going to secure us a place to stay in Anzaldúa, and I'll make sure you're fortified with extra troops from Mendez. Got it?"

Eva nods. "On it." Her happiness makes her look like she's floating as she scampers out the door.

Santos holds my gaze when it's just the two of us in the room. "You realize you just gave up the throne, right?"

I nod once, pretty sure the hard hit of that will come later. Right now, all I feel is relief.

Santos shuts the door. "It was the right call. I'm proud of you."

No one says that to me. I look down at my hands, examining them because those simple words make me feel entirely new.

Maybe I am new. Maybe this is our chance to start our future on the right path.

25

THREE CONVICTS
ADELITA

Saying goodbye to Tavita was difficult. She's so tough and steadfast in her decisions that to see insecurity waver in her gaze was enough to push me into her arms. I'm sure Tio Bruno didn't appreciate the dressing down I gave him in front of the soldiers, but it had to be done. Tavita is precious to me. Tio Bruno is the one who's going to answer to me if anything goes south.

Santos had a similar goodbye with Rafael, making him promise to be safe and to do all he could to bring Santiago home alive. The stress of knowing his twin is out there has been eating Santos alive. His stomach has been bothering him for days now. No matter how much I try to calm him down, he's still a ball of nerves.

"I can't do this," Santos said this morning, turning to

Tio Bruno. "I can't stay here while you rescue my brother. I need to go with you. Please, Tio Bruno."

Cruz and Tio Bruno went into the barracks, going back and forth on the pros and cons, but in the end, it was decided Santos would be useful going over to the island with the troops to help rescue his brother.

Cruz, Eva and I have been on the road for four hours now, and I sorely feel the absence of Tavita, Rafi and Santos.

I zero miss Tio Bruno.

Eva has been on her phone on and off throughout the entire drive, making arrangements in varying degrees of pleasant and clipped tones, depending on with whom she is speaking. Cruz and I have been pretty much silent, our fingers twined atop the console while he drives.

When we pull into what looks like a rundown collection of farms, complete with a caved-in silo, the sight doesn't inspire much confidence. "This is Anzaldúa?"

Tall rows of corn greet me, blowing gently in the breeze as if nothing eventful has ever happened here.

Eva chimes in from the backseat. "They lowered the barrier for you. Cruz, do you remember what to do?"

"Are you kidding me? It was my favorite part when we were little. Wait for it," Cruz answers with half a smile. He drives toward the field of tall corn, but he doesn't slow when he should.

I tense in my seat, leaning away from the dash. "Cruz, you're going to drive straight into the crops! Cruz, stop!"

Eva snickers at my panic while Cruz lets out a frightened cry, as if he's lost control of the car. I scream, but just when I'm certain we're going to crash into the thick stalks of corn, a sort of veil parts, and we pass through unencumbered.

Cruz and Eva laugh at my fright, which earns them both a scowl. "You could have told me it was magicked or whatever. How did they do that?"

The road is still filled with corn on either side of us, but the path we're on manifests a few feet at a time, leading us in at a downward angle. Pretty soon, the corn is well above our car, and we're driving below what I thought was ground level.

"It's a really solid trick of the eye. Mirrors and whatnot. Not even magic. It's how they keep people out. Only a few outsiders know how to access the entrance to their underground village."

My mouth pops open as light floods my view. "The whole village is down here?"

"Yep. They don't like outsiders, so they keep away from everyone by hiding underground. A few decades ago, they lost their chief and a fair amount of their people in a Kalku raid, so they relocated here. No need for a military. They're completely self-sufficient under here. They refuse to trade with us, because that would mean they'd be reliant on coming to the surface."

My mind reels at the new information. I'm not sure how to make sense of what I'm seeing. The ceiling stretches for miles. It's lit with lampposts that also serve to support the roof of the city. That's what I'm looking at —it's a whole city about half a mile wide and who knows how long. Stores and buildings line both walls, and the road we drive on is packed dirt.

Cruz pulls into a lot that holds a dozen cars, plus one empty spot, which I'm guessing is for visitors. Everything is spotless and brightly painted. It looks like a scene straight out of something decades ago, where most of the women are in dresses and the men are in overalls or jeans.

Cruz is stunning in the teal t-shirt that stretches taut across his burly chest, paired with navy fitted trousers that show off his tight backside. He's gorgeous, and I can't help notice how many eyes turn his way when he exits the car.

I'm nervous, never having been this far underground before. The air feels different as I get out of the car. It's... I'm not sure that it's denser, but there's a lingering chill I can't shake, and a dampness that coats my skin.

Cruz claims me quickly, tucking me into his side and tugging the brim of my baseball cap down to obscure my face. Rafael did my hair this morning, much to my amusement. He was doing his best to cheer me up through the crush of our impending parting. I love Rafi so much, goofball that he is. I'd even let him pretend he knows how to put my hair up if it gave me more time with him.

I miss him horribly.

I can't think about how badly I miss Santos. My stomach has been hollowed all day.

Eva takes my other side. She looks entirely different in tight black leggings, a matching halter top and a holster for her dagger strapped across her thigh. It's a clear display of "don't mess with me" that she usually doesn't have to wear.

She's nervous.

A man a few years older than me, maybe mid-thirties, trots down the street, his hand raised to signal us. He's lean but sturdy looking, with coffee brown hair that looks thick, even when he's not close up.

"That must be Salvador Gael," Eva says under her breath to us. "I've been communicating with him on this. The chief's son."

My chin jerks to her face. "You don't know what he looks like? You've never met this person before?"

Eva bristles. "I met him when I was a little girl, but Anzaldúa keeps to themselves. I'm pretty sure that's him. We have a code phrase to make sure, though." She lifts her voice enough to reach him. "The sun sets at dawn."

"Indeed, the waters rise in the east," the man replies, and Eva's shoulders lower. She nods to us. "It's him."

A significant measure of my confidence in the plan begins to plummet, but I have no choice now but to go with it.

Cruz postures as the man approaches. My boyfriend hitches me behind his back so his body shrouds me, just in case this man trotting toward us pulls a weapon. "We've come to see Don Luis Gael."

The clean-shaven man stops a few feet from us, noting our defensive stance. He holds up his hands. "Don Cruz, Lady Eva. It is good to see you both. I'm afraid Don Luis doesn't hold meetings anymore." He inclines his head to me as I peek out from Cruz's side. "I'm his son, Salvador. I'm glad you're here."

His manners are impeccable, but I'm not ready to relax just yet. His voice is uncommonly scratchy, like he's lived with a perpetual cold.

Cruz shakes his hand. "Thank you for this."

Salvador raises his broad nose and clicks his fingers, summoning a few men to come from the various buildings nearby, as if they've been standing around waiting for us.

That makes me nervous.

They trot to the car and start sweeping through it with a beeping handheld machine. One of them digs in the trunk and takes our backpacks out.

Eva protests when they open up her pack. "If you want to know the color of my underwear, it's proper to buy a lady a drink first."

Salvador smirks at her moxie. "I told you my men would search your car before we got you settled. We have to know if you've been followed, if you're being tracked, and what weapons you're bringing into the village. It's standard."

Eva grumbles under her breath, but she doesn't protest further than that.

The man with the beeping thing nods. "The car is clear of trackers. No listening devices, either."

"You heeded my instructions," Salvador praises Eva. "I didn't think your people capable."

So, it's going to start off like this.

Eva bites back just as hard. "Are those scanners from ten years ago? I didn't realize you had such modern equipment down here. See? Not all rumors are true,

Cruz. They're not a bunch of hillbillies who can't do basic arithmetic."

Salvador's brown skin gives birth to a full-blown smile. "We can do far more than basic math, I assure you."

Eva's hand finds its way to her hip, so I know she's done messing around. "Really? Because I see three people out in the open looking for one shelter, which you have yet to provide. Divide that by one pushy prince, and we're going to get exactly nowhere."

"Oo!" Salvador hoots, shaking his hand as if her words stung his fingers. "I don't remember you being this charming when we were children, Lady Eva. You've grown into your mouth quite well."

"*We* were never children. You were always an old man. Are you satisfied with your search now?"

He waits for his people to give a round of thumbs-ups before he nods. "So good to have you all here. Let's continue this banter somewhere more private. I'm afraid you've drawn many eyes out in the open like this. Keys?"

Cruz crooks his eyebrow. "No, thanks. I'll hold onto my keys."

Salvador's smile doesn't leave his brown eyes. "It's part of the deal. You take shelter here, and there is no trace of you anywhere but the rooms in which you'll be staying. That means your car goes. My men will drive it far away from us and leave it there until this is all over. Then, when you go to leave, we will fetch it for you." He motions to our black SUV next to the cars that are easily twenty years older than ours, and far smaller. "If the Kalku manage a breech, they'll have confirmation you're here if they spot your car first thing."

Cruz hangs his head. "I don't like this."

Salvador tilts his head to the side, his voice still carrying that perpetual rasp that makes him sound like a veteran smoker, rather than a man in his thirties. "I don't like visitors. Guess we're both going to have to make concessions. Keys, please."

Cruz clenches his fist, but then finally complies, dropping them into Salvador's palm. Cruz glares at his sister. "This is looking like a bad idea, Eva."

Eva doesn't argue, nor does she backpedal. "Where's our shelter, Salvador?"

His square jaw tightens, as if he doesn't relish the words coming out of his mouth any more than he anticipates we will enjoy hearing them. "You know what comes next."

Eva blows out a slow breath, then casts Cruz and me looks of apology. "I didn't tell you about this next part because you never would have agreed had you known."

My stomach drops. "What's going on?"

Eva lowers her head, but it's Salvador who chimes

in. "You wanted proper cover. Comply or find your way back out and take your chances in the outside world."

Eva casts Cruz and me apologetic looks. "He wants to cuff us for the onlookers." She jerks her chin toward the dozen or so people who have come out of the shops to gawk at us. "It's the only way to keep the villagers here from knowing royalty is visiting their tribe. We are three convicts who have turned ourselves in for crimes against Anzaldúa. The villagers won't bother gossiping about us beyond a day or two."

Cruz scoffs. "I don't think so."

Eva exhales and closes her eyes. "I'm trusting you, Salvador."

"You have good instincts, Lady Eva."

Her upper lip curls. "Stop using my formal title when it's clear you don't respect me."

Salvador moves behind her back, pulling cuffs out from his belt and gently pulling her arms behind her. His raspy words are quiet in her ear, but I can still hear them. "On the contrary. I respect you very much. Do you know how many from the Mendez tribe have tried to find refuge in our village through the decades? We turn them down every time. The fact that you've managed to secure something Máximo holds dear?" He jerks her arm, though I can tell it doesn't hurt her. It's more for show. "You have my undying respect, Lady Eva. And perhaps more than that."

What the...

Salvador runs his finger along her wrist. "For now, though, you're my prisoner. Let's give them a believable show. You turned yourself in for crimes against my tribe, and now I'm taking you underground where you'll be questioned and then locked up."

"I hate you so much right now," she growls through gritted teeth.

Salvador smiles. "That's exactly right. Good." He locks eyes with Cruz. "The cuffs don't lock. Understood? They can easily be pulled apart. It's all for show."

When one of Salvador's men moves toward Cruz, he stiffens. Eva shoots her brother a warning glare and he complies, staring daggers at Salvador.

But when a third goon in overalls puts his hands on my wrists, I can tell things are about to go south real fast.

"Not on your life," Cruz snarls. "Hands off her."

Eva turns to meet Salvador's eyes with none of her irritation, only concern. "She is La Ciguapa. My brother is owned by her. Tell your men to be careful, or my brother will not be able to hold himself back."

It's a lot of information for Salvador to process.

And frankly, I take issue with the "ownership" part of things. I don't *own* Cruz.

Salvador freezes, his mouth open as he gapes at me.

The man who was touching my wrists drops his grip and stumbles back. "Don't infect me!" he pleads.

This is embarrassing.

Eva directs the scene, which is no great surprise. Even in handcuffs, she has a commanding presence. "Salvador, put your hands on her back." Then to me she says, "Sweetheart, keep your arms behind you so it looks like you're cuffed." She meets her brother's eyes. "She is not cuffed, Cruz. No one is going to hurt her."

Cruz looks panicked for a beat, but then smooths out his expression with a solemn nod. "Okay."

Salvador lets out a low whistle. "What have you gotten us into, Lady Eva?"

"More than I can handle on my own," she admits. "Which way?"

The prince motions to the second shop on the left. "Just in here."

Eva's brows raise. "A candy store? Your interrogation room is a candy store?"

Salvador recovers a bit of his jaunty attitude. "The Kalku have no use for sugar, and even less patience for businesses dedicated to fun. If they get through, they won't target that store."

It's a well thought out system, to be fair. I didn't realize we would be sleeping in a sweets shop. My five-year-old self is rejoicing while my twenty-eight-year-old self is hoping for a firm mattress.

When we enter, Salvador gives the old woman behind the counter a cheery wave, to which she bows. "Don Salvador, do be careful. They look dangerous."

Salvador presses his finger to his lips. "Absolutely. Let me get them out of your hair."

The woman with a white chignon and weathered skin pushes a button behind the counter, and a display on the left jerks backward, revealing stairs leading into a darkened tunnel that slopes yet further down.

No. I can't go in there. Images of the dark pit plague my mind and stiffen my spine.

I don't like any part of this, but I have no choice. I swallow my scream as Salvador presses us down into the blackness.

INTO THE DARK
CRUZ

I hate everything about this. I can't see where I'm going. If Santos was here, I would feel better for a number of reasons, including that he can see in the dark better than anyone I know. "Where are you taking us?" I ask Salvador, now that it's just the four of us.

"Somewhere safe. There will be light soon enough, Don Cruz. Even my men will not know where I am hiding you. I trust them, of course," he adds, which makes me think he does not trust anyone. "I just want to give you what I promised: a hideaway. No sense in hiding you in plain view of the villagers, yes?"

There's a rattling, and Eva exhales. "You were telling the truth. Cruz, the cuffs break off easily."

Salvador's voice grows serious as I test my own, and

they effortlessly break apart. "I would not lie to you, Fair Eva. I would not risk war with Cáceres over this. If anything, I'm hoping relations between our two tribes are strengthened."

My nose crinkles, and I'm guessing my sister's does, too. "You don't deal with outsiders," I remark, my foot catching on... I'm not sure what. Is that a root? I manage to steady myself before I do a faceplant. Adelita locates my hand in the dark, tethering me to the earth. "Frankly, I'm surprised Eva was able to connect with you at all."

"Times are changing." Salvador is just nebulous enough to make me want to ask more questions, but his tone is closed off, so I know I won't get any answers out of him.

Adelita isn't quite so resigned. Gotta love her.

"It sounds like you're unhappy about that. You're helping us now, which is part of that change, I'm guessing." Instead of asking what he's talking about, she puts on her therapist hat. Salvador doesn't have a prayer now. "It sounds like you've got a lot on your plate."

Addy's voice is steady, but I can still hear her anxiety. She doesn't like the dark, and we're mired in it. Her fingers are chilly, so I press her hand between mine.

Salvador's pace slows, so we match his. "I suppose there's more on my plate than usual, though nothing that wasn't inevitable."

"It's tiring to brave your way through uncertainty for so long." Adelita's comment is thoughtful, but I can tell her mind is whirring, picking her words carefully to give us the information we need to trust this guy. "How are you being good to yourself through all the change?"

Salvador stops cold, so we halt as well. "I... I'm not sure. All of that will find its way back to me after the dust settles."

I expect her to argue, but all she gives him is a thoughtful "Hmm."

I want to fill the silence, but Adelita squeezes my hand to let me know she's at work.

Finally, Salvador speaks after he starts walking again, leading us with the sound of his footsteps. "You don't agree?"

Adelita's voice is warm without a hint of judgment. "I think *you* don't agree."

Bingo. I am so in love with this woman.

Salvador's voice turns sweet. "Lady Eva, it's alright. You're shaking. I didn't mean to scare you out there. I thought I explained the arrangement, but maybe I wasn't clear enough. Did the cuffs hurt your wrists?"

"No," she says quietly. "I just don't like being underground like this. There's not a speck of light. Take us somewhere better than this."

My sister is such a princess. Any other woman might

plead, but my sister demands. Even when she is afraid, Eva knows where she comes from.

I can hear the smile in Salvador's voice. "I know just the place."

Is he naturally like this, or is he flirting with my sister? I mean, she's an adult. She can do what she wants, but since he just had her in handcuffs, he should probably sniff elsewhere.

We turn down too many corridors to keep track of. I get the feeling that we're going further downward. The incline is so gentle, I didn't catch it at first. "How deep does your village go?"

"Deep enough," Salvador replies, answering me without answering a thing. That's annoying.

I'm so wrapped up in the sensations of the dark that I don't realize the shallow panting beside me at first. Not until Adelita's steps slow do I notice how feeble her grip has grown. "Addy?"

She drops my hand, and judging from the location of her voice, she's doubled over, hands on her knees. "Sorry, I just... It's different down here. Like being... Like being buried alive."

I want to glare at my sister for not prepping us for any of this, but I have no idea where Eva is standing. I quickly lower Adelita to sit on the packed-dirt floor, spreading my palm across her back. "Panic attack," I rule, sounding like Santos with my certainty. "Head between your knees, baby. It's alright."

Salvador gives us space while Eva drops to her knees on Adelita's other side. "This whole thing is more than you bargained for, huh. It's all to keep you safe from Máximo. No way would he think to look underground for you."

Addy's breaths come hard now. When I test her arm, there's no will to her movement. "Easy, now. You're going to make yourself faint if you don't slow your breathing."

"Can't!" Now her whole ribcage is contracting violently. "Sorry, I..." Then she leans heavily to the side, resting against me while she breathes like she's just run a marathon.

I lift up my chin in the dark. "How much farther?"

"Quarter mile. I know it's far, but it's the safest spot."

"That's fine." I lift the brim of my girl's baseball cap so I can kiss her forehead. "I'm going to carry you, okay? All you have to do is let me."

Adelita finally nods, though I can tell this effort costs her a portion of pride.

"A quarter mile," Salvador reminds me.

"I don't care if it's ten miles. If my woman can't walk to safety, I'll carry her there."

I ignore Salvador's chuckle. "La Ciguapa, indeed. I admit, I thought those were myths."

"She is the stuff of legend," Eva says with absolute seriousness. My sister might furrow under my skin from time to time, but she understands me.

"And you are the muse of poetry," Salvador replies to Eva.

Come on, now. What sort of correspondence did these two share?

"I'm sorry," Adelita says through too many labored breaths as I heft her into my arms.

Much better. Being in the dark is problematic for many reasons, one of them being that I have no idea if Adelita is alright. Now that I have her curled against my chest, propped up by my biceps, my own panic ebbs by noticeable degrees.

"There's nothing to be sorry about. You're in my arms. What could be troublesome about that? Other than the whole feeling like we might be buried alive part, it's not a bad day from where I'm standing."

Addy manages a wan chuckle. She cuddles into me, her head tucked under my chin. The hat obscures the scent of her hair, which usually grounds and surrounds me with peace. I won't admit aloud that I don't like this plan one bit. Since we're already mired in what I hope won't end up being misplaced trust, onward is the only way to go.

Salvador's voice is more respectful when he speaks

again several minutes later, breaking up the trek with polite conversation. "It's not far, Fair Ciguapa. I promise, this is the safest place I know of."

I don't expect light to appear out of nowhere, but suddenly a flashlight floods the path. The source is coming from my right.

My brows slam down. "You had that thing the whole time?"

Salvador doesn't look the least bit abashed. "Had to make sure we weren't followed."

"You trust your people that little?" Eva's question isn't too far off from what I was thinking.

"No, Lady Eva. Nothing like that. I'm a man of my word. I promised you a safe place where Máximo would never find your treasure. Taking every possible precaution is the very least I can do."

I don't like the way he says "Lady Eva". I can't put my finger on why, but it gives me the icks.

"We appreciate your discretion," Eva replies with a lilt to her tone.

She said that weird.

I turn my head to the side, yawning as a wave of sleep comes over me. It's barely dinnertime, yet suddenly I'm ten steps away from falling asleep. Maybe the air down here is denser or something, because it's harder for me to draw in a full breath. I stop and set

Adelita's feet down, but she's not steady enough to stand on her own. She stumbles and utterly collapses on the dirt floor.

I swear and try to pick her up, but my arms are heavy and clumsy.

Eva's footsteps stumble. "Salvador?"

I catch sight of Salvador's serene, resigned expression. "You'll have to forgive me for this. When I learned the other daughter of Máximo had been implanted with a listening device, I decided I couldn't take any chances. If La Ciguapa has been bugged somehow, I can't have her accidentally leading him here. No harm will come to you, Fair Eva, on my honor."

I'm barely processing his words, but they anger me all the same.

Even more frustrating is his patronizing hand on my shoulder. "Sit down, Don Cruz. You're about to pass out. I don't want you to squash your girlfriend." Salvador lowers my sister to the floor while she cusses him out between labored breaths.

He turns his back to me because he knows I'm too weak to stand and fight him. I take a swing, but it doesn't even connect with his side. My arm loses its fight halfway and falls limply as my eyelids droop.

In a last-ditch effort to protect my slumbering Adelita, I stretch my body over hers. Maybe I'm squishing her, but the fact that I'm heavy means he'll have a terrible time taking her from me.

My jaw goes slack as I watch Salvador lift my limp sister off the ground and take her with the flashlight in his mouth, down the corridor, leaving us in the dark.

27

BURIED ALIVE
ADELITA

My back is cold. Where is Santos? He always spoons me in the night, warming my spine. Cruz's hard body is under my hand, but the bed beneath us feels all wrong. The stiff support aches my shoulder. With every movement I make while stretching, more and more of the day comes back to me.

Biting back the sobs while saying goodbye to Santos.

Kissing Rafael's impish smirk.

The long road trip to... to...

Where am I?

My lashes open, introducing me to a room I've never been in before. Cinderblock walls should clue me in, I'm sure, but the damp scent surrounding me has never felt more foreign. I'm on my side on a packed dirt floor, cuddled up to a supine Cruz who's sleeping with his mouth open.

My movements are slow when I finally make the choice to sit up, taking in the room more clearly when I blink and rub my eyes. "Eva?"

My sweet friend is sitting with her back against the wall next to the door. Her eyes are wet. "Morning."

She's wearing the same black leggings and matching halter she had on before... before we... "What happened?" I ask her, unsure how we landed here, and where exactly "here" is.

Eva sniffles, wiping her nose on her sleeve. I wonder how long she's been crying. "Salvador drugged us. Landed us here. Not sure where we are, exactly. The door's locked. I led us straight into a trap. Now Anzaldúa has the Cáceres chief's son and daughter locked up, on top of the daughter of Máximo. My guess is that Salvador will barter with the Kalku to turn you over to them for the highest price."

I take a second to let her words sink in.

We're trapped underground in some sort of concrete-walled room. We were tricked by Salvador—promised safety while being swindled with a smile.

She sniffles and swipes at her eyes. "He wrote me poetry in our letters. For months, this gorgeous poetry. I thought I knew his quality. I was certain I could trust him." Her eyes squinch shut as her fists clench. "I'm an idiot."

I don't know what to say, so I crawl over to Eva and cuddle into her side, holding her hands so we can be scared together.

My absence alerts Cruz that it's time to wake up. My adorable boyfriend yawns and stretches, blinking the world into view with the same confusion I first wore.

When Eva explains her verdict, his eyes close, even as he sits up. "Weapons?" he inquires, a man of few words, especially first thing when he wakes.

Eva displays her empty hands. "They confiscated them, remember? We've got nothing."

I size up the steel door that looks like it locks from the outside. Still, it's an exit. When I lock eyes with Cruz, he nods, understanding what I'm silently asking.

I stand and try to reassure her as much as possible. "It's alright, Eva. You don't need weapons. You've got me."

She manages a watery smile, as if she thinks I'm speaking figuratively or being sweet.

But Cruz and I both know I'm the best tool for this job.

Cruz catches my insecurity. I don't want Eva to know my secret, but letting her remain trapped in here simply because I don't want to be found out is cruel and selfish.

My muscles are stiff, so I take my time stretching my arms over my head. "I'm going to need you to back away from the door, Eva. Give me a minute; I'll get us out. Though, what we're going to do once the door is opened, I have no idea."

"It's locked," Eva tells me lamely.

"Locks don't matter much. There's something you should know about Adelita." Cruz stands, shaking out his arms and legs, testing his balance and standing a few feet back from me beside his sister. "She was born with a blessing or a genetic flip or something. Not sure which."

"I'm strong." My summary is blunt and boring, but it is what it is.

I don't wait for Eva's reaction. I merely grip the curved handle and yank.

When the handle breaks off in my fist, I grimace. "Maybe I was the wrong key for the job. Crap. I'm sorry, guys." Cruz doesn't say anything to Eva's quiet questions. He lets me examine the doorframe. "I can shove through. It just may take me a few tries, and it's going to make some noise. So I'd be ready to run, if I were you."

Cruz nods, cracking his knuckles and rolling his shoulders, ignoring his sister's peppering of questions. "Go on, baby. We're right behind you."

I don't expect to get through on the first try, but I

really don't expect to hurt my shoulder when the door groans but doesn't open.

"Did you dent the steel? What the..."

I can't soak in Eva's amazement. I'm too perplexed that the door didn't rattle on its hinges. I try again, denting the door further. On the third try, I break through, but the door only swings two inches, stopping at a... "There's a dirt wall on the other side! The door was never meant to be opened." Before I can reign in my terror, a shout screeches out of my mouth. "They've buried us inside!"

Eva whimpers while Cruz starts looking around for other options. But it's clear to all three of us that the only way out is sealed in with dirt too thick for me to bust through.

Eva backs up until her spine hits the far wall. "I don't understand. How long have you known she could tear the handles off of doors?" Eva asks her brother.

Cruz doesn't miss a beat. "Long enough to know I can trust her. Nature trusts Adelita with strength like that. Addy is the one who lifted Santos' curse, you know. She yanked his curse axe straight out of the tree like it was no big thing."

Another whimper.

I've scared my friend. My sweet sister. I can't look at her, own up to what I am. I don't want to be scared of myself, of my strength, but some days, that's exactly what I am. So I pretend I'm not strong, pretend I'm not who I was born to be, so I can be less.

So I can fit in.

The realization of that simple truth hits me hard. Any competent self-actualized person knows that "fitting in" isn't a worthwhile goal. Yet I've kept myself quiet, my strength a secret, for most of my life.

My hand presses against the steel as I steady the rocking inside my soul. I cannot go back. I can't undo the unnecessary hiding I've always done. But I *can* live an authentic life with the people who are risking theirs to save mine.

I keep my eyes on the back of my hand as my voice begins to carry to Eva. "I was born like this—too much muscle. I think I scared my mom. I *know* I scared myself. Mom taught me to keep it all secret, so we wouldn't stand out too much. She was afraid of my father, but never said why. But we were always moving, always trying to keep out of sight." My fingers curl against the door. "She knew about magic and all this. She must've. She didn't tell me a thing about Máximo, not even his name. Nothing about the Kalku. But she knew. I'm certain of it. She rarely had friends because we moved around so much. She gave up everything for me, and she died because Máximo wanted to steal me and take me to his island." I swallow hard. This story is hard to stomach. "Tavita's mother was murdered on the same day. Her captor took her to Máximo's island, but Santiago was sent to snatch me up. He didn't follow orders, though. He blessed me when he saw me. Told me I would only be as strong as I was gentle. He put a cap on Máximo's asset, so if Máximo ever got his hands on me, any attempts to break my spirit would also shred away my strength. It was a smart move, really." My head hangs. "But since then, my strength has grown. Sometimes I'm worried I'll sneeze and break something important by jerking too much."

Cruz is keeping up, for which I'm grateful. "Your muscle grew because you're naturally gentle."

There's a beat of silence before Eva speaks. "Which means you're even more of an asset to Máximo now. Santiago letting you go and keeping you away from Máximo made you all the more valuable, because the gentleness wasn't tortured out of you."

I wince at her words and cringe at the truth in them. "I didn't think of it like that, but you're right. Whatever Máximo wanted me for two years ago, I'm more than strong enough to do now." My eyes close, because I can't bear the thought of any of this. "I'm a therapist," I protest weakly.

I didn't hear Cruz's footsteps, but his hand touches

my back, rubbing soothing circles along my spine. "That's right. That hasn't changed. You're just taking a little extended leave, is all. You're still you, even down here."

I lean into his touch, letting it ground me when life feels doomed and out of control.

"You should have told me all of this," Eva chides, but she doesn't press more than that.

The three of us startle when the wall to my left rumbles. The three of us step back, and even though we just discussed at length the breadth of my muscle, Cruz stands in front of us, shunting us behind his wider body. Though we have no weapons, Cruz unlocks his knees and prepares to pummel whatever it is that's making the wall shake.

My mind takes a second to register the sight as it unfolds. The wall has no door, but the thing slides like a patio entrance, creating its own opening. There isn't a wall of dirt behind it, but a tunnel, revealing Salvador with a grim expression. He offers no greeting, only his presence, which is such an oddity that I can't form proper words or accusations.

Salvador steps into the room, risking our wrath. His hands tuck at the small of his back. "Máximo's curse is that whatever he most wants will always be just out of his reach. He most wanted you, I'm guessing, dear

Ciguapa, which is why you were out of his reach, given the help of this Santiago person." Salvador's eyes fall on me as I peer around Cruz's shoulder. "Máximo wants his curse removed. That's what he needs you for." His eyes fall to Eva. "We cannot let that happen. You were right to bring her here, Lady Eva. Now that I know what it is you're protecting, I can truly help."

Cruz isn't interested in logic or conversation. His fist flings out like a boulder, clocking Salvador across the jaw and dropping him to the dirt.

Yes, we're off to a great start.

28

BROTHERS AND DOGS
RAFAEL

Santos is a machine, in both the good and the bad sense of the word. He lost his patience when we stopped to eat and refuel before we reached the harbor, though I'm sure not many could tell. Santos isn't one to inconvenience people with his feelings, so only I noticed his pacing and the tightness of his jaw, which is akin to when Cruz would lead the way with his abrasive shouts.

Santos is doubly motivated. He wants to get to the island and free the captives, sure, but this is his assumedly dead twin brother we're talking about. Plus, every hour he's away from Adelita is one that makes him more agitated.

La Ciguapa. I never knew it was real, but now that I have that tidbit to factor in, it all makes sense. I want to tell Santos to take a breath, but it would be a wasted effort. He belongs to Adelita, who luckily is a good person that doesn't abuse his devotion.

The water is choppy the farther out we go. This was the best chance at getting peaceful waters this week, so we set out without proper training this morning, and it showed. The blue of the waters feels like a slap in the face, what with all the crimson that's been spilled, leaking out over the green of the harbor. I don't like that we left behind a trail of bodies. A team from Mendez will be by to help with cleanup so our fallen soldiers will be respectfully taken back and buried with their ancestors.

There's no swell of victory, no straightening of our spines. We are all exhausted and weighted by the near-escape we just endured.

That's what it was: not a victory, a near escape. The words keep banging around in my head. We were ninety-six. Now we are six.

We were outnumbered, plain and simple, outmatched and outfought. The fact that there are six of us still standing is incredible, to say the least. There is no mourning, not yet, anyway. There is only the mission, only the goal.

Only the fire in Santos' eyes.

We expected the Kalku to come out of the woodwork

when we reached the harbor. There are always some guarding the way to Máximo's island. But this was overkill.

"They knew we were coming," I say aloud while Santos and one of the soldiers rows.

Our men weren't prepared for their agile and overly flexible fighting style. Only Santos and I were prepared for it, because that's what we've been up against while out on the road. The Kalku aren't civilized; they fight differently.

And that lack of training cost us dearly.

It scared me when one of the Kalku used his dying breath to blow into a wooden flute he had tethered to a rope around his neck. It was a low yet rallying tune. I don't understand its purpose, but even the memory of the sound sends shivers through me.

"That flute. Did you hear it? What was it for, like to signal a retreat for them or something?"

Though I posit the question to all the survivors, Santos knows I'm really talking to him. He knows why the Kalku do what they do.

Santos' face is stern. "It's to summon the Massacooramaan."

Tavita clutches the side of the boat. "I remember back to when I thought all of this was a myth. Our best bet is to hope we get to the island undetected."

Tio Bruno's jaw tightens as his hand cups Tavita's shoulder. "If we come across the Massacooramaan, he will die, just like the Kalku we slaughtered to get here."

Santos meets Tio Bruno's eyes with a gravity that doesn't sit well with me. Dread coils in my chest when Santos finally speaks his mind. "Your bravery is foolishness." His body is tight as he rows. "I can only hope you're as right as you are arrogant."

Tio Bruno scowls at Santos. "Do you have something you want to say?"

"I told you our soldiers weren't ready for a fight like that. You dismiss my fighting style because it's not yours. You forget that you're fighting savages, not men with morals and a family to go home to. Too many of our people died out there today. It could have been Rafi. So yes, I hope you're right that the Massacooramaan will be simple to slaughter. I have no plan for fighting one."

Tio Bruno hisses as Tavita ties a shred of material around his thigh—a scrap of shirt taken no doubt from one of the fallen. He was stabbed and it hasn't clotted yet, but he's in good hands.

Santos doesn't let up, which tells me he's been pushed far past his breaking point. "Your soldiers gathered around Tavita to protect her, but that was unwise, as I tried to tell you on the way here."

Tio Bruno hisses at the pain in his leg. Santos is

poking a bear that's already having a bad day. "You'd rather I not protect the daughter of Máximo?"

"She didn't need it. The Kalku knew not to touch Tavita. She was our saving grace. When they came near her, they faltered, afraid to touch La Ciguapa, afraid Máximo's daughter might get accidentally killed in the fray. They are more afraid of Máximo than of you."

I wince at the blunt nature of Santos' summary. I motion between Santos and Tio Bruno. "If you two don't find a way to hug and get past this, there will only be four survivors left, because I'm about to throw you both overboard," I tell them. Of course, I would never do that to Santos.

Tio Bruno? Well, that's a different story.

Tio Bruno's voice rasps when he speaks. He's winded but steady. "Santos, take a break. Alonso can row for a bit."

Santos isn't disrespectful enough to argue a direct command, but I can tell by the defiant gleam in his eyes that he wants to.

"Explain why," I instruct Tio Bruno. Santos might be new to speaking up for himself, but I know what he needs. Though he can talk aloud now, Cruz and I will forever be his interpreters, guiding him through the rough social waters.

Tio Bruno doesn't have the energy to glare at me. He

connects his gaze to Santos' once the other guy takes the oar alongside Alonso. "You need to recharge. I haven't seen you in action in a while. I think I forgot how well you fight. You took down a quarter of them by yourself, easily. You're so pumped with adrenaline that you'll crash before we get to the island. Then you'll be exhausted when we'll really need you to step it up. You've earned a break."

I can tell it's a struggle for Santos to speak his mind, but when I nod, he finally does. "I don't want a break. I want to find my brother. I want to get back to Adelita and Cruz."

"I understand, Santos, but..."

I can tell Tio Bruno has more to say on the subject, but Santos is too jacked up on the high of the fight, and lets rebellion finally punch out of him. "No, you don't. You have dinner with your brother every night, and you barely look him in the eye. You leave before dessert and you hardly say anything unless it's related to work. Santiago is my family. You don't know what that is."

I purse my lips, holding in a hearty "aw, dang!" that wants to slip out.

Tio Bruno looks as if Santos just slapped him across the face. I can see several arguments wrestling for first place on his face, but when Tavita sits on the bench beside him at the back of the boat, his entire demeanor softens. "Then tell me, Santos."

I can't believe I'm hearing a soft reply from the stalwart military commander.

Tio Bruno's hardened edge softens the longer Tavita is near him. "Tell me what we're searching for. To me, it's a mission to go to the place we've never dared and free captives we didn't know existed. We all assumed it was just Máximo on the island before Tavita educated us. So for me, it's a chance to free captives and possibly even take down Máximo. You'll need your strength for that."

Santos looks disgusted, though props to Tio Bruno for spelling all of that out without attitude. "All of that is nothing. What is the point of killing Máximo?"

Tio Bruno balks at him. "He's evil, Santos. You, of all people, should know that."

Santos wipes his sweaty face on his shirt. "Yes, and what of it? Evil is everywhere. If there is nothing good we're saving, then all we're doing is fighting a losing battle. Killing evil? Fine. More will pop up to take its place. There is no shortage of evil in the world. But there is only one Santiago. You are sailing across the sea to cut off the head of a monster that has an infinite number of heads. It's noble, but it's meaningless if that's all it is."

Tio Bruno's jaw ticks, but when Tavita smooths her

hand down his arm, his indignation evens out. "I think my goal is a good one. Why is yours better?" It's incredible to see the effect Tavita has on Tio Bruno's entire demeanor. I'd thought Cruz learning manners was a miracle, but if Tavita can quell Tio Bruno's stern temperament? I'll do whatever it takes to keep her in Cáceres.

"Because good is always a better reason than evil." Santos' eyes unfocus, watching the waves. "Santiago took my beatings whenever he could. When I made a mistake, he would tell them it was him, and they would hurt him. It was wrong of him. They could see right through the lie, too, but they punished him anyway right in front of me because they knew the worst pain for me would be to see my brother suffer." Santos' fists clench and loosen over and over as tension ratchets through his body. "Your brother suffers because of your distance, but you don't care. You are too busy fighting evil to tend to the good. So the good dies from neglect. You are scared to hug Don José. You forget what you are fighting for, so you fight for nothing."

I freeze at the boldness in his words. Maybe he's starting to take Adelita seriously with all of her "act or accept" talk. Seems like he's done accepting Tio Bruno's crappy attitude.

Tio Bruno lets out a low whistle. "Well, look who found his voice."

I balk at Santos' gall. I don't correct his overstepping. I wouldn't dream of reeling in this gold. I only wish I had a recorder. "Your poetic bits sometimes got lost without your voice, Santos. That was really awesome."

Really awesome? I sound like an idiot.

But Santos doesn't mind that he outthinks and now outspeaks me ten-to-one. "I have much to fight for. I have my brother on the island who needs me, and my family in the village who loves me." He says that last sentiment with withered confidence, as if the act of claiming love aloud is audacious and scary. Still, he owns it as best he can, and I couldn't be prouder. He's come such a long way.

Tio Bruno shocks me by not responding with a resounding "shut up" or something to that effect. Perhaps our surly uncle is growing, as well. I'm guessing we have the woman who's stroking his arm to thank for that. "Is Santiago as opinionated as you?"

Tavita speaks up with a chuckle. "Santiago is a poet, much like Santos. He's got something to say about everything. The world will be new to him once we take him to Cáceres, so we should all remember to tread lightly. Some of the other island slaves have been there far longer." A shadow falls over her eyes. "They might prefer to die with their master. Fear of him is the only love they've ever known."

That statement stuns me, hollowing out my stomach.

It could have been me. I always remember how lucky I am to have been rescued before the Kalku stamped out the best parts of me—making me think fear and love are one and the same.

Something bumps the boat, knocking us all to the left. I grip the side, my eyes scanning the waves for signs of what could have knocked us. I'm not thrilled that this unsteady footing puts us at a clear disadvantage.

But part of me knows what it is. Everyone on our boat understands what we're dealing with, even though we've never seen him.

Alonso stands up and opens his bench, yanking out a life preserver. He shoves it at Tavita. "Here. Put this on." All the soldiers scramble for life preservers, including myself, but Santos doesn't bother.

That's a good thing, I guess, because there are only five life preservers and there are six of us.

I try not to be frightened when the boat rocks violently, but a whine of distress sneaks out. "Santos, what are we dealing with?"

Santos moves Tavita to the center of the ship and gently but firmly sits her on the floor of the boat. It's wet, but that hardly matters now. Another hit from below knocks a wave into our vessel. The sun is hanging low in the sky, doing us little service in brightening our optimism.

Santos keeps his eyes on the water. "Massacooramaan is bigger and taller than any of us. There are versions of him I've heard where he's ten feet tall, and others say he's fifteen feet tall."

Carlos, the sixth survivor, snipes at Santos. "Great. How accurate is any of this?"

Santos turns his chin slowly to face the soldier. "Not many live after meeting the Massacooramaan. And it's hardly practical to measure a man who rises from the water. That wooden flute the Kalku blew was to summon him. He heard it, and judging by the waves picking up without the breeze to make them grow, he has come for us."

"He works for Máximo?" Tio Bruno asks.

"The Massacooramaan was Máximo's greatest experiment at the time. Martino was his name, back when he and Máximo lived in caves as part of the Kalku. They were like brothers, some say, closer than any two could have been."

Santos' eyes flick to mine, and in his gaze, I see his pledge to me. To Cruz.

The three of us are just as close—sealed together by an unbreakable bond.

Just like Máximo and Martino.

"Martino would do whatever Máximo asked, even volunteer himself up for Máximo's experiments. By the time the two broke off from their cave and Máximo rose to the leading position in the Kalku, Martino was unrecognizable."

Santos watches the waters as they grow choppy. "Martino needed someone to call the shots, so he didn't mind being mutated. He was the only one Máximo allowed to follow him to the island, but even that had its bitterness. Martino is not allowed on the island, but instead he acts as a sentry. His lifespan was lengthened by Máximo, which sounds like a blessing, but all Máximo did was make him his eternal slave. Now he's too strong for anyone to attempt killing, and not even nature will make him succumb. His brotherhood got him enslaved. His loyalty was his downfall."

I can feel my heartbeat in my cheeks. The stories are so very similar, yet with distinct differences. There is nothing Santos and I would not do for Cruz, just like Martino held nothing back from Máximo.

But the difference is that Cruz looks after us. He values us. He made us his brothers.

Still, I can see how seamlessly the whole system could crack and turn toxic.

Santos points toward a green light in the distance. "That's the Luz Mala. If any of us survives, that is the thing which must be destroyed. Without it, Máximo is mortal. So first we destroy the Luz Mala, putting out its light. Then we can go after Máximo."

Tio Bruno holds Tavita's hand, his thumb rubbing across hers. "I didn't know all of that. I've never even known the Massacooramaan's real name." He motions to the beam of green light in the distance. "I've never understood the Luz Mala. I mean, I know it's linked to Máximo's immortality, but I wouldn't know the first thing of how to destroy it, or how it came to be in the first place."

Santos doesn't clam up. I'm so stinking proud of him. "All I know is Kalku lore. The Luz Mala was made by Máximo to hold unknowable treasure. But apparently it's so potent that it can't exist on the mainland. So Máximo is on the island with his experiments and his immortality." Santos' chin dips down. "They say if you are drawn to the Luz Mala, it's because your spirit is aligning with Máximo's. Some would leave the cave and try to sail to the island because they loved Máximo so much. But they always died. The Massacooramaan kills anyone who tries to get to the island."

"Even his own people?"

Santos nods. "If you can make it past the Massacooramaan, then you are worthy. Many have died for the illusion of worthiness." His eyes go out of focus. "When I was first liberated from the Kalku, I worried I would be drawn to the island, that I was evil, and would have no choice but to join Máximo."

This guy breaks my heart. "Santos, there's isn't an ounce of selfishness in you. The only thing that's forcing you toward the island is the promise of rescuing your brother."

"Yet still, here I am, drawn toward the Luz Mala. Drawn in the direction of evil." Santos turns his chin before I can argue, holding my gaze with an expression that seems to say, "Rafi, you don't know all that I've done."

It's true that I don't. I never want to know, either. Most of my childhood with the Kalku has been blissfully blocked from my memory.

"Best get this over with. We are about to find out if we are worthy."

Ice laces into my spine. "What?"

"Martino!" Santos calls out. The boat rocks as if in response. Santos raises his voice. "That's right. I know your name. I know what you've done. You can eat me, but it won't erase what you've done. There are scores of people who know your sins. They know why you really lurk in the depths."

I'm cold from head to toe with fear. "Maybe goading him on isn't our best move."

Santos' eyes are cold. If he was man before, he is savage now. "Máximo stole my brother. Today I steal his." He grips the edge of the boat, his teeth catching the light of the fading sun. Vengeance glistens in Santos' golden eyes. "I am worthy."

Adelita is not here, so there is no emotion in his voice. She amplifies his heart. Without her here, the sweeter parts of him go silent.

I swallow hard. "You sure you know what you're doing?"

"Máximo didn't. When he took Santiago, he didn't realize he was inviting death to his doorstep. This monster is the guard dog. Máximo tore my family apart? I will dismember his."

I look out onto the water, worried a huge squid or something is going to pop out and take us under.

Tavita finally speaks up. "Máximo speaks to Martino. The Massacooramaan."

Everyone goes still. When she doesn't elaborate, I prod. "I'm going to need more."

"When he's troubled, he goes to the water's edge and speaks to a man who's not there." Tavita doesn't look affected or disturbed by any of this. On the contrary, her forced calm is a blanket that covers over any spike in emotion. I can see that this is her method of survival. "A few prisoners tried to escape, but whispers about the Massacooramaan taking them to the bottom of the sea stopped me from trying the same route. I never saw a sea monster, but I saw enough of their remains floating to the shore to stay put." She points to Santos. "On the island, they say he's fourteen feet tall, for what it's worth. A big, hairy man with teeth like knives—pointy and overly long." She shivers, and Tio Bruno tucks her into his arms. "He capsizes boats and eats the people inside."

Tio Bruno's hand touches on the nape of her neck. "You got in the boat. I asked you to come with us to the island to help us, and you're here. You should have said no to me."

A muscle in her cheek flexes. "No. This is where I belong. One way or another, I was headed back here. I'd rather do it before Máximo kidnaps my sister. I didn't want to wait to make the trip after he's already got his hands on her. Best end this now. Adelita is sweet. She cannot handle life with Máximo. Santos is right. Fighting evil with vengeance is no reason to cross an ocean. Protecting goodness is the only thing that should motivate us."

She shivers again, but it's not due to the breeze that

sets my teeth on edge with its chill. The waves keep us in place now. No matter how hard we row, the water corrects our course, making sure we don't reach our destination.

I might vomit. I'm deadly on land in a fight, but at sea I have no idea how to wage a war.

"Act or accept," she says, repeating Adelita's credo. "There are only so many injustices I can accept."

Santos is ready. He draws his knife when the boat is bumped again.

I think I'm prepared for the sight of a tall, hairy yeti or whatever poking his head up out of the water, but when the eyes find me, a new chill slices through any semblance of bravery.

He's enormous and muscular beneath the hair that's inches long all over his body. Massacooramaan's teeth are too lengthy for him to close his lips around them. True to Kalku tradition, his teeth have been shaved into sharp points, like all their top warriors. There are two bottom teeth, though, and they jut upward so high, I worry they'll scrape across his nose. He's hideous, but more than that, he's focused on us.

We're locked in a standoff, with the Massacooramaan manipulating gravity so he doesn't move at all as the waves grow more frustrated, slapping against our boat. I want to attack from a distance, but I highly doubt my dragon's fire would catch on something that's soaking wet. Plus, if my dragon comes out, it'll wreck the boat.

"Stay in the boat and keep your heads low," Santos instructs. I assume he's talking to the others, but he pushes on my shoulder to force me down.

Tio Bruno ducks his head, but that's the most he'll obey.

I feel like a child with my knees curled to my chest. We have no plan for this. We weren't expecting to have numbers this few.

Santos rests his hand atop my head to keep me in place. His fingers comb through my hair, soothing my angst because he loves me. Even in this moment of impending bloodshed, Santos will always and forever be my brother.

When Santos speaks, his voice carries out over the water with the bravery of a man who's not afraid to die. "You will let us pass. I do not have the patience for Máximo's dog today."

I cringe, wondering if taunting the Massacooramaan is the best way to go.

I'm surprised when the Massacooramaan speaks in a low, clear cadence. I guess I expected unintelligible gurgling or something.

"I am no one's dog."

"Yes, you are. I recognize what you are because I was a dog once, too. I was a cave slave, but I got out. Yet here you are, a dog even now, moments before your death."

The words hit me hard. I was rescued as a kid, sure, but I was being groomed to become a cave slave. I was chosen to be nothing more than their dog. When my family turned away from me after I was rescued, I was certain there was nothing for me, no chance at a good life. Then Don José took me in and made me his son.

No one rescued Martino, so the disgusting ways of the Kalku were all he had to aspire to.

A growl ripples out of Massacooramaan. The waves smack so hard that water sprays into the boat. Both Alonso and Carlos look like they're seconds away from vomiting.

"You dare speak to the great Massacooramaan like that?"

Santos remains in control. "No, I'm speaking to *Martino* like that. Máximo has my brother on his island. I will be bringing my brother home today. I do not wish to take down a fellow dog, but if you do not let us pass, you'll leave me no choice."

Tavita whisper-shouts to Santos, "Are you crazy?"

But Santos pays us no mind. When the boat rocks so hard it nearly tips in response, Santos grips my hair and turns his chin toward me. "Stay in the boat, no matter what. I love you, Brother."

I don't have time to respond before Santos hurtles himself overboard, diving into the rough waters with nothing but his knife clutched in his fist and my heart tucked inside of his.

29

A BROTHER'S DEATH
RAFAEL

"Santos!" I shout into the twilight. I'm on my feet the second Santos jumps into the water. His arms cut through the waves that only grow more intense the farther he swims.

Though he told me to stay in the boat, no way am I being benched so I can watch my brother die at the hands of the hairy Massacooramaan. This can't be how his life ends.

But when my hands hit the ledge of the vessel, Tio Bruno grips me around the waist and tugs me back. "Don't you even think about it. Losing Santos is a hard enough hit. We cannot lose the both of you."

"Santos!" I shout for my best friend, but I can only see the determination in his strokes.

The Massacooramaan smiles, revealing his janky,

overgrown teeth the closer Santos gets.

Suddenly, my vision tunnels.

I don't know if my dragon can swim, but I'm about to find out.

My temper hits a crescendo, and Tio Bruno's arms fall away. My waist bulbs as I leap over the side of the boat and splash down into the water so my dragon's weight doesn't capsize the boat.

At least my life preserver manages to stay in place around my neck.

As I pull myself through the water, fighting each swell with muscle that's willing to fight to the death, I catch sight of scales rippling across my forearms. My nose elongates so much that I can see it stretch out half a foot from my face, forming into a snout.

I breathe in long gusts, in and out, willing my shifting to pause to the half-mutated being I used to be able to become. My snout doesn't retreat all the way, but it's not nearly as long as it was a breath ago.

And just like that, I feel a click inside my body.

I'm partway shifted, my human legs kicking out behind me.

I did it. I'm still mostly me, with a few enhancements.

The Massacooramaan's growl cracks across the water, but I'm well past my fear of him. I only want to save Santos. The two feelings are linked, I'm sure, but Santos is my only focus, the thing that's driving me forward once I get my shifting under control.

Santos reaches the monster before me, and that's the moment I know true fear. It's a pup going after a bull. My speed picks up, but so does my zeal to protect my brother. He did not survive all he's been through only to die at sea. There is no part of me that is willing to accept that I won't be coming back to the boat with him.

Massacooramaan zips to the side, swimming clear around Santos, as if he doesn't care about doing battle with him at all. My stomach drops when I realize Massacooramaan is heading straight for the boat, his eyes locked in on Tavita.

I turn to intercept his path, but Massacooramaan moves his arm in my direction, and a giant wave knocks me off course.

If anything, I would think he would help us to the island, being that we're clearly traveling with a daughter of his master. But when he approaches, his words burble out just loud enough for me to hear.

His low cadence chills me all over again. "Máximo wants you."

Tio Bruno shields her with his body, and two other soldiers do the same. "He's never going to get his hands on her again!" Tio Bruno shouts.

Massacooramaan stops only a handful of feet from the boat, as if he's simply come by for a pleasant chat. "I let her pass my waters once before because she was going away from the island. But you are taking her back to Máximo?"

I swim harder, but I don't understand his tone. He sounds almost disappointed in us for bringing her along.

Tio Bruno answers. "She knows the island, so she's going to help us take Máximo down. Step aside, or we'll have no chance but to take you out, too."

Massacooramaan tilts his head to the side. "She cannot go back. Máximo has lost his mind. He will turn her into a monster this world cannot handle. If you do not turn back, I will take her to the bottom of the sea. Better that than what her father has in store for her."

Tio Bruno looks just as confused as I am. When another wave pulses in my direction, I'm distracted by the fight with it, and drift further away from the boat. He's going to exhaust me to death, keeping me at bay until I run out of energy.

Tavita pokes her head out near Tio Bruno's shoulder. "What plans does he have for me? What is so terrible that it scares even you?"

"He wants his daughters to set him free."

Tavita angles her body as far forward as Tio Bruno

will permit. "What does that mean? Free from what? From his curse?"

My lungs ache with the effort of fighting the waves that keep pounding in my direction. I'm getting nowhere, treading and struggling with my whole body to get closer, but making zero progress.

Massacooramaan's only reply is a shake of his head while I try to keep my nose above water. "Go back to the mainland. Máximo wants his daughters. He cannot have them. I made the mistake of letting the Kalku bring you here two years ago. Never again will I let a daughter of Máximo pass through."

"We have to go," Tavita explains, borderline pleading with the sea monster man to understand. "We can't let this continue on. Whether we go over on our own or not, Máximo will come after us. He's already tried to bring me back with Adelita."

Adelita's words come back to me full-force: "Evil only needs permission to thrive." Tavita is making it clear to our foe that we will not abide this a moment longer. She is just as brave as Adelita.

"I will drown the one who can tear out his curse axe before she ever reaches the island. It is the only way."

Everyone on the boat gapes at the sea monster. Tavita recovers first. "It sounds like we have the same mission. We have to stop Máximo."

Good, Tavita. Make him see reason.

"No. By going to the island, you're giving Máximo exactly what he wants."

My stomach sinks. In that simple statement, I can tell we're not going to dissuade him.

My whole body rebels as I fight harder, panting now and losing any hope that I might out-pummel these waves. I need to get to them. My animal keeps struggling to come out, but I know that with his shorter arms and heavier weight, there's no amount of effort that could propel my dragon through the water.

I'm fighting with too many things... and losing.

A wave rises up behind the boat, stretching whole stories into the air. The terror strikes so much fear into my chest that I forget how exhausted I am in a moment of sheer marvel.

Tavita's scream is the only thing I hear over the roar. As it crashes down on their heads, the splintering of the boat sickens my stomach. The waves I've been wrestling with now double, taking me under for half a minute at a time.

I punch my head through the surface seconds before my lungs burst. The twilight doesn't give me much help in illuminating the scene, but I'm able to pick out the remains of a broken boat floating by.

The Massacooramaan doesn't look joyful at all at his

victory. He glances over at the green beam of light—the Luz Mala, and I catch true regret tugging forlornly at his hairy features.

I dive under the water, hoping to catch glimpses of the soldiers, of Tavita, but it's too dim to see properly.

But then I make out a shape—half a shape, perhaps. It's long with a plume of what I assume is blood jutting out from the end.

When I swim closer, shock rattles my bones.

It's the lower half of a person, freshly severed and drifting toward the bottom of the sea.

I knew the Massacooramaan was rumored to be able to capsize boats and then eat the sailors, but at no point had I actually visualized how horrific that inevitability might be.

We are down to five survivors now.

When I resurface, something catches my eye that I don't expect.

Santos swims with dogged purpose as if he's not fatigued at all. I don't even see him blink as he thrusts up and wraps his arms around Massacooramaan's neck from behind, dragging the monster off his balance. He's got the back of Massacooramaan's head pinned to his shoulder while the monster flails.

I swim toward them, now that the Massacooramaan

is too distracted to pelt me with his best weapon. Santos is insane to attack without backup.

Gotta love him.

Massacooramaan lets out a howl of pain as Santos wraps his arm around and stabs his dagger straight through the man's eye.

Even though defeating him is what we've set out to do, the savage nature of Santos never ceases to surprise me. I cringe at the sight, accidentally jerking backward instead of rushing to help.

Another stab, and the Massacooramaan is completely blind. His howls are the stuff of nightmares, and I'm fairly certain they will haunt me for many nights to come.

My dragon recedes a little, now that it sees Santos isn't drowning. My bulbous belly coming back in makes it far easier to maneuver through the water, but I'm only halfway to Santos when he jerks the dagger out of the monster's second demolished ocular cavity, and plunges it through the man's heart.

Massacooramaan's mouth opens in shock, but no sound comes out, or if it does, I'm too far away to hear it.

I reach them seconds after Massacooramaan's body gives up its fight.

Santos lets his conquest go. The hairy body drifts toward the bottom of the kingdom it once ruled.

I feel a myriad of unquantifiable things. We could have worked with the monster, perhaps, if we'd found a way to be more convincing. He didn't want to follow Máximo's lead anymore. He'd finally found a way, after more than a century, to stand up to the madman who led him down this path.

In his death, I see Santos. I see myself. I see every citizen in Cáceres who goes along with the status quo rather than standing up and declaring loudly what the right path should be.

"Come on," Santos says without an ounce of emotion. "Let's get you some debris to float on. We can't swim the rest of the way without support."

He's winded, but he doesn't stop until he's taken me by the arm and dragged me toward an orange spot in the night. "Tio Bruno, hold tight together. I'll find the others."

Tio Bruno doesn't heed Santos. Instead he reaches for Tavita, whom I spot just a few meters off.

Carlos was the one whose top half was eaten by the Massacooramaan. Alonso looks to have been maimed beyond repair, all life gone from his face as Tio Bruno drags his body toward us.

It looks like we are down to four survivors now. I can only hope it's enough to take down Máximo.

Alonso's life jacket is removed and shoved over

Santos' head, giving his body and lungs a break from the fight of trying to keep his head above water. Santos shudders, but that's the most he'll carry on. "There are other things in the deep. The fresh blood will draw them in soon enough. Let's go."

And with that, there are four of us, left floating in the middle of the sea.

Tavita whimpers, which triggers Tio Bruno to pull her closer. Their life jackets make for an awkward embrace, but they manage. "Let's go," Tio Bruno directs, his chin aimed in the direction of the island.

We swim as well as we can with the jackets on, but until we come across the oars floating in the water, our progress is slow and far too labored. When the oars give us something to cling to, our legs propel us forward until finally the island comes into view through the night sky.

"Volcano," Tavita points out. "That's where Luz Mala is hidden. We go there first, then we go for Santiago. Then we hunt down Máximo."

"No," Santos argues. "My brother comes first."

Tavita pushes back just as firmly. "If we die fighting Máximo to get to Santiago and the other slaves, then the world still has to live under the fear of him. We free the world first, then if we die liberating your brother, at least the rest of the world will be better off without

Máximo being able to draw his immortality from the Luz Mala."

I can tell Santos doesn't like this plan, but he bites his tongue through any arguing he'd like to do.

It's a long time that we push through the water. I've lost track of the hours, but the moon is nearly overhead by the time our tired bodies reach the shore.

I make out trees that are far taller than those in the village. They're coated with a shiny gloss that reflects off the moonlight. It's almost pretty, but I don't have the wherewithal to mention that aloud.

The island is far larger than the village—maybe four times the size, but it's hard to tell in the dark. It's quiet here, with the ocean lapping at the shore, eating tiny blond specks of sand and sending them into the waters that never sleep.

It took all my effort to get here, but now that I made it, I feel vastly underqualified to traverse through this place that's entirely foreign to me.

Santos stumbles to his feet on the sandbank, but I don't have that kind of energy.

"Sit," Tio Bruno insists. "If we go in half-cocked, we'll be taken down before we make it halfway to the volcano. Collect yourselves. Take stock of your weapons."

Santos complies, but again, it's clear he's itching to get to his brother.

I have one knife that managed to stay with me after all we've been through. One knife that's useless to me because exhaustion has set deep in my bones. My back rests against the sand, my chest heaving in both relief and terror.

Cruz, my heart cries. *Adelita.* I miss the four of us in bed, cuddled in close like children waiting out life's storms.

I want to go home to them. I want to leave this awful place that's lit by a green glow from the Luz Mala.

I miss my family, but I know that to keep them safe, I need to see this thing through, and end Máximo once and for all.

Though I know I'll be roused far too soon, my eyes close, stealing a few minutes so I can dream of better times.

When I awake, we will defeat Máximo, and I will have my family back once more...

...if this journey doesn't kill me first.

Love the book?

Leave a review.

If you don't leave a review, Rafael dies.

AFTERWORD

Enjoy a free preview of "Wicked Hearts", book five in the *Savage Hearts* series.

BONUS CHAPTER

BONUS CHAPTER
HALF A MONSTER

Santos

Our feet drag across the sand that seems never-ending. Since traversing the sea to get to Máximo's island, we're still shaken from our encounter with the Massacoora-maan. What's sticking in my mind isn't the sea monster's sharpened teeth that climbed up to his nose, or the fact that his entire body was covered in inches-long shaggy hair, nor the sight of him at probably around fifteen feet tall. What's haunting me is the fear I saw in Rafael's eyes. He wasn't afraid *for* me, he was afraid *of* me. I'm sure of it. I have lived with him long enough to know the difference. They all resisted my fighting style in the beginning, and for the most part, I've learned to adapt to their militaristic ways. Cruz, Rafi and I have mostly met in the middle—a little savagery married with a brush of calculated force. But when my death would mean my twin brother would remain imprisoned and Adelita would be without my protection, the savage in me came out.

Maybe it was too much to plunge my dagger into the ocular cavities of the Massacooramaan.

I'm still not sure I regret it. Two more soldiers are dead now, because I couldn't reach the Massacooramaan sooner and end him before he destroyed our boat.

None of us have mentioned that even after we destroy the Luz Mala (the source of Máximo's longevity and power), and free the prisoners, we have no way of getting home. We floated the rest of the way here on the remnants of our boat.

We're just as stuck here now as the slaves we came to liberate.

But that's not the thing to dwell on. One massive problem at a time.

Tavita insisted the best plan is to get to the Luz Mala, because if we fail at rescuing Santiago, at least we will have destroyed Máximo's chances at living forever.

I guess it's solid logic, but I'm a storm of restlessness inside. All I want is to find my brother and go home to Adelita.

Adelita.

I've known she was La Ciguapa from the beginning. No one could have enchanted me so quickly and permanently with the simplicity of a small smile. Having it confirmed by Tavita hasn't changed anything for me. It's being separated from her for this long that sends a dagger of pain through my side. Every step away from *mi Corazón* has been a difficult choice, but I've made it nonetheless.

I understand the balance that must be struck when you've been sucked in by La Ciguapa. Adelita could ask me for anything—even my own soul—and I would give it. The fact that I can leave her to find my twin brother is proof that Adelita will not ask me to be less than I am. My heart is more important to her than any desire to force me to tend to her whims. She knows this is the quest I must take, even though it tortures us both to be separated like this.

It's another reason why I want this job finished as quickly as possible. I need to get home to her. There's a gnawing ache in my gut, like a critter is trying to scrape away at my stomach lining until I get back to her arms. I still can't believe it's me she welcomes into her bed every night, that I am the one who gets to hold her when she is overwhelmed. I am the luckiest of all men because she runs her fingers through my hair. When I can't make sense of the world, she is kind and patient.

My bones feel wrong, moving further away from Adelita, but my soul cannot tolerate being separated from Santiago a minute longer than necessary. I'd thought him dead, ignoring the pull that told me I needed to find him. I saw him get stabbed by one of the elders in the cave the day I was liberated.

We were both supposed to die that day.

It's the practice of the Kalku to kill off the slaves if the cave is compromised, but Cruz and the others got to me before the deadly blow could be dealt. I was cursed with muteness, so any mourning I felt at my twin's supposed passing was silenced.

It's the habit of Cáceres to kill off the Kalku and free the cave slaves. They take us back to the person's previous home or to a hospital and leave them to what they hope is a better life.

But I'd had no previous home, since I had been with the Kalku since I was a baby. I am fortunate Cruz and Rafael took me to Cáceres. Their love kept me alive. Kept me sane.

They gave me a new family on the day I lost my brother.

It's what should have happened to both Santiago and me, but only I lived through the raid.

Santiago, had been killed off, or so I thought. But Tavita informed us that my twin brother was taken to Máximo's island to do the evil maniac's bidding.

"I need to stop," Rafael admits, though I know he is speaking up for Tio Bruno's sake. No one is bold enough to tell the military man that he should be thinking about retiring, so Rafi takes the label of being the weakest link to give Tio Bruno a break. We've all seen better days. The fight with Massacooramaan came on the heels of the slaughter of half our militia.

Tavita's spine straightens when we stop to sit. She stands over us, like a mama bear guarding her rambunctious boys. She sniffs the air, so I follow suit. My human nose picks up the typical scents: sand, ocean, bark, foliage. But there's a note of something else that's organic and new to me. I can't quite make it out.

I shift into my wolf, stick my nose to the sand and then poise it in the air.

Animal, that's for sure. Though this one smells… off. Like dog, only stronger.

I tilt my head up at Tavita, wondering if her stiffened posture is because she smells the same thing.

When she senses my gaze is fixed on her, she bends down and runs her fingers over my fur.

Because she is Adelita's sister, I allow it.

Tavita angles her chin away from the Luz Mala—the green beam of light we have been walking toward. "You smell that, too? I was afraid this might happen. We might be too late to stop Máximo completely."

I sneeze at her.

"We might have to be quieter, moving forward. Máximo had a plan, back when I lived on the island. He liked to abduct men that the Kalku had mutated into cadejos (or shifters). Máximo would take their animal and experiment on it, changing it. I don't know how he did it, but his goal was to make their animals into monsters."

Rafi's neck shrinks as he stretches out his legs across the cool sand. The night air breezes past us, but it's Rafi's words that send a chill up my spine. "I was one of the first cadejos in the cave when I was little. Or, I was supposed to be, anyway. I was liberated before they could finish my animal."

Tavita turns to him and finally sits in the sand. "That must have been awful. Is that why you halfway shifted in the water?"

Rafi snorts. "Nah. I'm not all that sure if my animal can swim, so I was purposefully trying to keep him from coming out. But when he went after Santos, I had a hard time holding back." He fixes his eyes on the volcano that contains the Luz Mala inside. It's still a good few hours' distance away. "Adelita kissed me a while ago, and it did something to my animal. It healed him.

Completed him. So I can be full-on monster now, if I want to."

Tio Bruno and Tavita gape at his confession. Tio Bruno's nostrils flair. "It's a fine time to tell us that! I saw your snout grow, and that was news to me. I thought maybe I was seeing things, or that I didn't remember what your animal looked like. It's been a long time since you've shifted in front of me." He tilts his head skyward. "Adelita did this? She pushed your animal along, and now it's a full-blown dragon? What else do we not know about this girl?"

Rafi smirks but still watches the volcano. "I would imagine there's a great deal we don't know about her. Cruz, Santos and I know more because we took the time to earn her trust. And honestly, she didn't know she could heal people with her kisses, much less complete my transition."

Tio Bruno's volume rises. "What?"

Rafi grimaces. "Did I not mention that? It's how she was able to heal my dragon. She kissed me, and her mojo did its thing. But she kissed Santos' face before that. That's the *real* story behind his scars smoothing out."

Tio Bruno frowns and stares at me, even though I'm in my wolf form. "So I guess the story you fed us before about finding a special cream was a giant lie."

Rafi holds the flat of his hand parallel to the ground and tilts it from side to side. "Would we call that a giant lie?"

Tio Bruno rolls his eyes and then addresses me. "So Adelita kissed your cheek, and your scars healed?"

I bob my head.

Rafi claps his own shoulder. "She healed up a gash from a knife fight, too."

Tavita bites down on her lower lip, stepping back. Her limp has always been there, but it's worse after all we have been through to get to the island. "This is bad. I thought I understood why Máximo wants Adelita so badly. Sure, he wants his curse lifted, and she could make that happen. But she can also complete a cadejo's transition. If a shifter's animal has been badly mutated, she could heal them. Complete them. That's nearly every slave on this island. Máximo wants an army of cadejos, so he takes ones the Kalku have already made. Then he mutates their animal to make it more deadly. If Adelita can kiss one of them that's half-mutated and complete their transition?" She shakes her head. "I don't want to know how lethal Máximo could become."

Rafi shakes his head. "My dragon isn't more deadly. It's complete now. I'm able to fully shift."

"Making it more deadly," she finishes.

Rafi ducks his chin. "Oh. I guess you're right. But my

animal isn't crazy or anything. My dragon would never take orders from Máximo."

Tavita touches the spot behind her ear where Máximo had implanted a listening device. We had it removed, but I know it haunts her. "You don't know that. If Máximo wants something, he takes it. Father sacrificed someone so he could control my actions and override my better judgment. Who's to say he can't do the same to you, once he gets his hands on your dragon?"

I swallow hard, green light shining out of the volcano.

Tio Bruno's hand finds Tavita's back. Now that it's only Rafi and me as his audience, he doesn't hold back his attachment to her as much. "What are we up against? What sort of animal is Máximo making?"

Tavita swallows hard. "You'll know it when you see it. The animal is nothing like I have ever witnessed in nature. They are not themselves when they shift. In their human form, they're cave slaves under Máximo's rule, but they still have their wits about them. They can still think for themselves. But in their animal form, they only do his bidding. If you see one, you're probably as good as dead."

My head jerks back and I let out a sneeze of protest. No cadejo is going to best me. I mean, honestly. Not to toot my own horn, but I just took down a sea monster in the middle of the water. Plus, I've never heard of a shifter's animal not obeying its human counterpart. That's ridiculous.

The caution in Tavita's eyes gives my bravado pause.

When we start toward the volcano again, I keep to my wolf, my nose working overtime to track down any encroaching enemies before they attack us.

Tio Bruno offers his arm to Tavita, compensating for the limp that seems to stem from her hip. He is good at being there for her, silently helping her without bringing attention to his kindness or her shortcomings.

I like them together. Tio Bruno is insufferable apart from her.

I need to find to Santiago. I need to get him out of here.

No matter who I have to take down, I will bring my brother home.

Read "Wicked Hearts" today!

ABOUT THE AUTHOR

USA Today bestselling author Mary E. Twomey lives in Michigan with her three adorable children. She enjoys reading, writing, vegetarian cooking, and telling her children fantastic stories about wombats.

While she loves writing fantasy, dystopian, and paranormal tales for her readers, Mary also writes romance under the name Tuesday Embers, and cozy mysteries under the name Molly Maple.

Visit her online at www.maryetwomey.com, and sign up for her newsletter, so you never miss a new release.

www.ingramcontent.com/pod-product-compliance
Lightning Source LLC
Chambersburg PA
CBHW010316100726
47906CB00006B/1021